I0570365

BLOOD TIES A BROKEN HEART

CASSANDRA HAWKE

Blood Ties a Broken Heart
ISBN # 978-1-78430-489-8
©Copyright Cassandra Hawke 2015
Cover Art by Posh Gosh ©Copyright February 2015
Interior text design by Claire Siemaszkiewicz
Totally Bound Publishing

BLOOD TIES A BROKEN HEART

Dedication

To my daughter, Georgie
for our shared love of horses

Chapter One

The white canvas awning put up by the funeral director did nothing to cut the searing heat of the summer sun as Rylee stood silently by the hole in the ground that would soon hold her godmother's coffin. Her heart ached with grief for the woman she considered her second mum. They had lived on opposite sides of the country for the last ten years, but distance had done nothing to weaken their closeness. She clenched her brother's sweaty hand in a tight grip, taking what little comfort she could from the contact. A damp band formed where her little black hat was crushed onto the damp tendrils of her dark wayward curls and perspiration trickled between her breasts, making her feel sticky and uncomfortable.

Her high heels sank into the green cushion of buffalo grass, tightening the stretch on her calves and making it difficult to keep her balance. She stared with desperate concentration at the rosewood coffin balanced above the gaping cavern of earth. The one single stunning pink rose wreath that decorated it was already wilting in the vicious sting of the sun fired by the forty-degree day. She wished the torture over, as her tears dried on her cheeks. The priest droned on, but Rylee barely heard the ritual words that were supposed to provide comfort and respect. Her thoughts were filled with how her beloved Aunt Aileen had died of a heart attack, alone, amongst her horses, as she tried to maintain her once thriving business. If it hadn't been for the St. Clair siblings she would have been here and the stables would have been successful.

The scent of toasting eucalyptus tickled at her nostrils and she took a deep breath of burning summer air filled with the scent of gums, the sea and the roses and knew she was home. The priest intoned the Lord's Prayer and was echoed by the mourners. Rylee glanced from under her eyelashes to examine who had attended this final farewell. The mourners made a small gathering—a few strangers, friends of Aileen Jones, and a half dozen well-known faces from the equestrian fraternity. Rylee sighed, such a sad end to endure for a special lady.

She halted her scan of the gathered mourners. He stood at the back of the crowd, different, but the same. She was attracted to, and yet repulsed by, the familiarity of his features. A barrage of emotion slammed into her chest, clenching her heart in a vice of anger entwined with unrequited passion. Only Regan's relentless grip on her arm ensured she stayed upright as her knees buckled under the unexpectedness of his sudden appearance. Her throat, already dry and rasping from grief, now burned with sandpaper dryness as she tried to swallow. She stared at him, mapping every contour of his beloved face, the tinge of gray at the temples, the new lines around his eyes. She wanted desperately to reach out and touch him, to feel the smoothness of his tanned skin under her fingertips, her body sizzling inside with unbridled sexual need. In her mind, she heard his voice, smelled his scent, and remembered the taste of his mouth on hers. Her chest clamped tight against the sobs that threatened to choke her.

A whimper of agonized misery escaped from between tightly compressed lips, and Regan squeezed her hand, thinking to comfort her in her grief. Beyond responding, she clutched frantically to the last threads of composure as she stared silently at him.

Ashford St. Clair, the love of her life, the destroyer of her dreams. Her beloved, who had turned his back on their love when he had very publicly put his sister before Rylee in a nasty tangle of horse doping, misguided loyalty and lies.

Then he was gone, farther back in the gathered mourners. She searched the unfamiliar faces surrounding her with a despairing need to find him, to catch another glimpse of the man she loved. The urge to break away and push through those congregated at the graveside screamed at her, but she held still, for Ashford St. Clair could never be part of her life and she would never disrespect her godmother in such a way at the very last moment of farewell.

As the priest conducted the final rites, Rylee acquiesced to Regan's gentle urging to walk forward and scoop up a handful of the red soil offered and sprinkle it on the coffin. Frozen in the moment of seeing him, Rylee robotically went through the motions of saying her personal goodbye, thanking the mourners and speaking to all who came for refreshments back in the chapel. She anxiously scanned the crowd, but he had gone.

The man she had fallen in love with ten years ago — Ashford St. Clair. The man who had done such wrong that she had fled across the country to the bosom of her family, knowing that single act made him forbidden to her. It was inevitable that she would see him now she had returned home, but did it have to be so soon, so unexpectedly and cause such burning anguish? She had fled after the incident, taking her smashed heart with her in the hope that it would heal. She still yearned for him, her feelings just as intense, painful and unrequited as they had been so long ago.

She would never be able to forget the sight of Ashford St. Clair standing by his sister's horse with an empty syringe in his hand days before an important three-day event in which she would be competing. The reverberation down her spine from the terrible roar that had burst from her godmother still echoed in her ears and the flushed, guilty expression on his handsome face while he had tried to conceal what he had in his hand remained clear in her mind as if it had only happened yesterday. When she had seen his sister Arden skulking in the shadows, Rylee had stayed silent, despite knowing immediately that Arden was to blame. The love she had for Ash had quivered under the resulting scandal but not died, even when she had been forced to cut all ties with him lest she be implicated and lose her standing in the equestrian world.

The following month she and Arden had fought it out in the eventing arena with Arden driving her horse, Lord of the Manor, unmercifully over the cross-country course. Her burning ambition to win had ended with a nasty fall that injured Arden and left Lord of the Manor with a broken leg that had cost him his life. Rylee had taken first place, but she'd lost the desire to compete that day and had sunk into a deep depression. At her godmother's encouragement, she had fled to Tasmania in the hope she would forget Ashford and heal from the betrayal of their love.

* * * *

When Rylee told Regan she had seen Ash at the funeral, he just shrugged. "Look, sis, you are just going to have to come to some arrangement between your head and your heart over that bastard or you're not going to make a go of this place, and that will be a kick in the neck for Aileen Jones, considering what she has left you."

"I know I have to, Regan, but I just don't know how."

"Well you better figure it out real quick, Ry, because next weekend is the International three-day event and you should be there and you are bound to bump into him or his cheating sister. Get your shit together, sis."

Rylee shot a savage glare at her brother before she turned back to shuffling through a pile of dusty tack. She knew he was right, but she wasn't going to admit it.

"Fine. Bury your head in that dead tack for now — but think, sis. What you are going to do."

"Leave me be, Regan," she muttered.

He stomped out of the dusty storage room, and she heard him saddling up one of the horses.

In an attempt to avoid facing Regan's pragmatic attitude to Ashford St. Clair, Rylee moped around the tack room for a couple of days on the pretext of sorting and salvaging, but she made little progress until she pulled out a polished wooden trunk. It had a latch but wasn't locked. As the contents came into view, she lost the grip on the lid and it crashed shut. She stood there with her hands resting on the top of the trunk, gasping for breath, tears welling in her eyes. After several long breaths, she re-opened the chest and stared at the contents. Her trophies, ribbons, her riding gear all done up in plastic with mothballs, her boots, her bridles and saddle. Everything from those days. There were several photographs. She picked up the one featuring her and Ash the day they had come second and third in the CCI2* event. They looked so young then, smiling and excited. Rylee ran her fingers over Ash's features, touching his mouth and remembering the feel of his lips caressing her own. They had been young then, and naïve in believing their dreams of riding for Australia would come true. *Things had been simple then.* She replaced each item as she had found it, shut the lid and pushed the trunk back under the bench.

* * * *

Friday dawned warm and still. Rylee fiddled over breakfast and Regan finally lost his patience with her.

"So are you going or not? Rylee, damn it, you can't keep moping around here, never going out, not eating. Aileen Jones would not approve. That I can tell you," Regan shouted.

She looked up at her brother, knowing he was right. This is not what Aunt Aileen would have wanted for her, but how did she tell Regan it was not grief for her godmother that kept her at the stables, a virtual recluse. How could she tell him she still loved the bastard who had caused her so much pain and how even going to the event as a spectator would tear her into shreds?

To sit quietly by while Ash's baby sister and her ex-best friend, Arden, galloped past on her newest horse, free to compete because Ash had taken the rap for her in the doping scandal was almost more than she could stomach. His four year ban had long since finished, but the mud had stuck and his reputation had been so damaged he had never competed again—nor had Rylee. She had been so disillusioned by her best friend's methods to win, she had refused to be part of it. It still hurt to have given up her dream to ride for Australia in the Olympics, but she knew she had made the right decision.

"Well, sis? You really should begin networking and all if you intend to fulfill Aileen's dream of re-building these stables back to their heyday," Regan yelled at her.

She looked up at her brother. "I don't know if I can face it. I'm not ready."

"For Christ's sake, Rylee, it's been ten years. You chose to stop competing. There is no point crying about it now."

"I know, Regan, but it hasn't changed anything."

Regan stomped away across the room then turned to face her. "God damn it, sis. You still love that bastard, don't you?"

She nodded. "I can't help it, Regan," she wailed. "And it wasn't him that did the dirty on Aileen. It was his sister."

"So bloody what," Regan shouted. "He took the rap for her, so where did his loyalty lie? Obviously not with you."

"I know. Arden always came first and always will," Rylee muttered.

"Okay, so you know where you stand, so get your shit together, Rylee. Unless you do, you will never get these stables up and running and I didn't come all the way from Tasmania to watch you smash yourself against a drop kick like Ashford St. Clair until you break into a million pieces."

She stared up at him, flinching under the anger in his words, shying away from the thought of never being with Ash again, totally unable to comprehend that he didn't deserve her love.

"The pieces might not go back together this time, sis," Regan informed her. "And I don't want to lose you to the black dog again. Okay?"

She nodded. When she had arrived in Tassie, she had been so deep in depression many had feared for her sanity, but the gentle love of her stepmother and her siblings kept her afloat until she could cope again, and she'd pulled through.

Making a huge effort, she finally lifted herself off the sofa and headed to her room to change.

* * * *

Immediately the noise, smells and sights of the event was a panacea to Rylee's soul. She realized then just how much she had missed the equestrian scene—the horses, the people and the excitement of competition. But even with the familiar atmosphere, she was on edge. Glancing at huddled groups, peering past horse floats and studying the horses warming up, she moved randomly amongst the crowds, every nerve tingling with anticipation.

Despite the unhappy memories she so wanted to see him, even knowing it was going to be a painful experience, and she would probably throw herself into his embrace regardless of the consequences.

She longed to hold him, to retrieve that warm tingling sensation they had shared when he'd touched her. Even though she knew he wouldn't be riding, she couldn't resist glancing at each dark-haired male on horseback that passed, remembering as if it were yesterday his relaxed easy seat and steady, gentle hands on the reins. She tried to shrug off her hyper-vigilant demeanor and bring her constant flinching under control as she bumped into strangers and acquaintances alike, but she failed dismally. He was here. Soon she would face him. Then what? She had no idea. Did she have the strength to calmly greet him and walk away or snub him even? She doubted it. Even now she trembled inside with a greedy expectation of his nearness. One touch and she would be lost in an abyss and unable to find a way out. That one touch could never happen if she was to stay immune or at least have the strength to pretend he didn't matter anymore. She tried to pull her straying thoughts back in check. *I am not here to see Ash. I am here to drum up some business.*

With a new sense of purpose, she did the rounds, deliberately seeking out those who had attended the funeral in the first instance then tentatively renewing old acquaintances. Most seemed welcoming and accepting of her plans for the stables. Many asked if she was going to resume riding. No one mentioned the St. Clairs or the unfortunate incident. It hurt that Arden St. Clair had emerged from that situation untouched by the scandal. For the first time since she had set foot back in Adelaide a fortnight ago, Rylee was glad to be back, and a sudden determination gripped her. She would fulfill Aunt Aileen's dream to restore the stables to a well-respected equine establishment.

With some idea of who was competing, she made her way to the beautiful historic Victoria Park Racecourse Grandstand. She barely recognized it with the renovations bringing it back to its former glory. There was quite a crowd, and she found a seat about three rows from the front. She had a good view of the whole arena and she had her binoculars to get a closer look at the actions of the horse and rider as they moved through the required movements of the dressage tests.

There were some stunning horses involved today, mostly thoroughbreds, but she had seen a couple of warmbloods being prepared for the CCI4* competition. What she was actually seeking were newcomers to international eventing, perhaps those needing the facilities she could provide.

Rylee made herself comfortable as the first of the competitors entered the ring. A young rider from Victoria, Jaynee Amos, on her ten-year-old gelding thoroughbred, Felka Abbey. Rylee watched every move of horse and rider, almost feeling each action. Part of her pined for what she had lost by giving up competing.

In between each competitor she scanned the grandstand, every nerve ending twitching in anticipation of his appearance. If Ash didn't come before, he would when Arden made her appearance. Rylee knew that dressage was not Arden's forte because she was too impatient and she never seemed to quite be in harmony with her mount. Rylee wasn't sure she wanted to watch Arden compete but something held her frozen to the seat with a tortured gaze focused on the arena as she heard Arden's name announced. Rylee glanced around the edge of the arena and the grandstand but could not see Ash.

Her first ride was a Clydesdale-thoroughbred cross, Cockatoo Ridge Jackaroo. The big gelding had beautifully smooth gaits and his transitions were fluid. As the pair proceeded through the tests, everything seemed technically perfect, but there was something missing—an edginess about the horse and just the slightest hesitation in paying attention to Arden. That lack of harmony was reflected in the score given, and Rylee could see Arden was far from happy as she rode from the arena.

* * * *

When Rylee returned from having some lunch, she settled back in her seat to wait for Arden's second ride. She had bought an equestrian magazine to look through to see what suitable horses might be available to add to her small collection. She had identified an un-catered to niche in the market of promising young riders wanting to compete without having to invest immediately in their own horse. With a couple of good horses, she could attract these younger riders and improve her reputation at the same time. She closed the magazine when Arden's name was announced.

Arden entered the arena at a collected canter and halted to salute the judges. Her second horse, Copper River, was an Australian stock horse x thoroughbred—a stunning chestnut. The horse seemed edgy, even as it moved off in a collected trot.

Rylee looked around, convinced Ash would be there somewhere, observing his sister's progress. There he was, in the front row of chairs, leaning forward as if to get a better view. Her chest tightened, cramping her breathing, as she sat motionless in her seat. Rylee studied the curve of his shoulders and the back of his neck. Every nerve ending tingled as if she was touching him with her fingers, gliding through the silken strands of dark hair. Even as she sucked in tiny breaths, she imagined she could smell his cologne. As he straightened, she watched the muscles in his back and shoulders undulate and flex beneath the thin material of his shirt. Warmth ignited in her and her pussy burned with a primal craving and moistened with anticipation. Her arms ached with the need to hold him. Her soul called to him.

She appraised him so intensely with hungry eyes. He had already turned before she realized, and she couldn't break her gaze from his when she caught him staring up at her his expression filled with longing. With a slow, sensuous stroke, he wet his lips and the tiniest hint of a smile tugged at the corners of his mouth. Rylee watched his chest rise and fall in an agitated rhythm, and his body become more erect. He examined her with his intense stare, the probing look, assessing every inch of her body, lingering and exploring, in a way his hands never had. She squirmed under his blatant scrutiny, fighting the fiery passion racing through her body, making her pussy and the flesh around it throb with arousal. The soft swell of her breasts above the scooped neckline of her tee tightened and she was aware of the push of her nipples against the laciness of her bra. Without breaking eye contact with her, he rested his hand on the back of the seat and sensuously stroked the wood with his fingers. Rylee shivered. Ash brought his hand up and ran it through his hair as he looked down at his lap, then back at her. Instinctively she reached up and touched her own hair and tucked a couple of wayward curls behind her ear. She struggled to breathe.

He rose and shuffled his way along the chairs, never breaking her gaze. She watched him, spellbound by his nearness, his sexiness and her longing. It was only when he began to climb the steps that the sexy haze of need shattered into bitterness and reproach. Rylee leaped out of her seat, scuttled sideway to the aisle and sprinted down the stairs. She paused and looked over her shoulder. Ash stood in the adjacent aisle. As he got closer, she could see that his expression was filled with wretchedness. He mouthed the word 'please' as he held his hands out wide. She gave a tiny shake of her head, tore her gaze from his and fled down the steps. *I can't do this. To face him like that – to feel like that.* Torment ripped through her, the pain of her rejection assaulting her heart and rending it in two. Sobs forced their way from her chest, catching painfully in her throat before escaping as distorted yowls and squeaks. Tears blurred her vision as she stumbled through the strolling crowds, horses and taped off areas. With as sudden *whoosh* the emotion drained from her and she halted in the shade of a tree. She stood panting. *What the hell was I thinking? To let him get to me like that. Ten years hasn't changed a thing. How could I be so stupid to think it had?* Rylee pressed her forehead against the rough bark of the trunk and sniffed. *Damn I am better than this – stronger. If Ashford St. Clair wants to moon over me, let him. There can't be anything between us while he maintains the lie.*

Angry at herself for letting the encounter totally demolish her interest in the day's events, she rinsed her face with water from a drinking fountain and walked back to grandstand, her head held high, her back straight. She took a seat a little higher than before and pulled her hat well down over her face. One quick look confirmed that Ash had not returned to his seat.

Rylee made herself comfortable and enjoyed the remainder of the dressage, eventually becoming so absorbed she even forgot to watch for Ash.

* * * *

Determined to make the most of the second day of the event, Rylee headed into town early. Today was the cross-country section of the event and her favorite. It was also Arden's best discipline because it was fast, challenging and not without its dangers.

Rylee found a place to observe the cross-country near one of the water jumps. The course seemed challenging and spectacular, and with the length of it, Rylee didn't expect to bump into Ash as she had yesterday.

Arden came round on Copper River, executing the ditch and brush fence with precision and style. Arden appeared confident and her horse willing as she went flying past. As Arden disappeared behind the trees, Rylee realized how tightly she was clutching the bunting. Rank bitterness swept over her for what could have been as she made her way to the water jump. At this stage of the course Arden's would be tiring and the jump needed to be treated with respect or they wouldn't clear the pelican on the way out. It would give her great pleasure to see Arden unseated into the water. Rylee remembered how much Arden hated getting dumped and wet. As she waited for Arden to come around, memories of that last competition crowded into her head. It had been her decision to give up competition and even to this day accepted it was the right decision for her, but the last couple of days had stirred her competitive edge and memories of the rewards she got from competing at a high level.

She heard Copper River coming and turned to watch his approach. The horse seemed to be struggling, breathing hard as Arden pushed him at a cracking pace. He cleared the wide log and landed well balanced in the water. Arden urged him on and he jumped the raft cleanly, but he took one look at the black and white pelican shaped jump and veered to the right, almost unseating Arden.

She brought him around, obviously furious from the way she yanked on the reins and kicked the tired horse's sides. He came again, baulked and backed up. Rylee smiled. *That's forty penalty points. Just one more refusal, Copper love – just one more as she's out.*

Rylee almost felt guilty when Arden urged her horse at the bizarre-shaped bird jump and Copper River, snorting and shaking his head, planted his feet and refused to attempt the jump. Arden was almost ejected from the saddle and over his head, but to Rylee's disappointment, she stayed seated. Nevertheless, she was eliminated from the competition.

* * * *

With Arden now having no chance of joining the top riders in the winner's circle or qualifying for Olympic team this time round, Rylee felt relatively happy as she trudged back to the car to meet Regan for lunch. While she had struggled to sleep last night, she had thought long and hard about Ash and determined where she stood as far as he was concerned. There was no denying her sexual attraction to him. It had never waned, but there could be no relationship between them. Nothing except a complete retraction of the doping lie could bridge the chasm that lay between them. But to Rylee it was more than just his public profile as a horse doper. He had claimed to love her and yet when it came down to a choice between her, the truth, his professed love and his sister Arden — Arden had won. It *hurt*. Rylee felt betrayed, almost as if he had cheated on her. And the fact he'd thought it wouldn't matter offended her even more. Yesterday he had caught her off guard. He wouldn't do that again because from now on, she would be fortifying herself against the torrent of lust that had swamped her unguarded heart when she gazed into his eyes.

With her head down to shade her eyes from the glare of the sun filtering through the trees, she hurried round the last of the tents and toward the car park. She heard him before she saw him. The familiar deep, husky timbre of his voice resonated along her spine. She shivered and looked up to see him just a few feet away, perched on the bonnet of a car, his arms folded across his chest, his handsome features partially hidden by his Akubra. Dressed casually in taupe dress shorts and a lemon button-through shirt, he was as handsome as ever. Rylee froze in the skimpy shadow of the tent, watching him. She didn't recognize the man he was talking with, but their conversation seemed intense.

Afraid of being seen, she backed up a little into the canvas wall of the tent, not taking her eyes off him for a second. He appeared tired and stressed, with a restlessness about him that had not been there before, and Rylee wondered what had happened to him while she'd been gone. She hadn't forgotten the shame that had consumed him after the incident.

Nausea suddenly rushed over her and the world spun in a dizzying spiral. She clutched the ropes that held the tent in place with a desperate grip and cursed her failure to wear a hat. She had to stay upright or there would be no dignity for her in their inevitable confrontation. As she made to sneak around the corner of the tent, the ground wobbled and she swayed. The rope grazed her palms as she crumpled to the grass, blackness shut out any coherent thoughts.

"Rylee, open your eyes. Are you all right?" Ash asked, gently bathing her face with his wet hanky.

He cradled her head in his hand, the scent of his aftershave tickling at her nostrils as he brushed her hair off her face with tender strokes of his fingers. Tears trickled from under her eyelids as the pain of loving him seared through her. She opened her eyes to meet his concerned look and almost shut them again to cut out the sight of him.

He assessed her with a dark, unfathomable look. She wondered if he could read the emotions in her expression and decided to leave himself room to retreat if she berated him with contempt or fury. He smiled, suddenly and unexpectedly—a lazy, sexy smile—full, pouting and undeniably kissable. The small crow's feet that crinkled in the corners of his eyes enhanced the smoky seductiveness of his stare. Rylee remembered the taste of him and shivered with need.

"Rylee," he said again.

"Ash," she responded, struggling to get even that single word out of her constricted throat. *So much for guarding against the rush of lust or is it something more — love, perhaps?* Even to ask that question speared pain through her and she knew in that moment she could not run from the competing feelings deep in her heart. She hated him for what he represented, and yet, she loved him for the man himself.

"Are you all right? Can you stand?" he asked, already reaching around her to lift her from the ground.

She nodded and let him assist her, luxuriating in his touch for just a moment—a precious, dangerous moment. "I'm fine, Ash. Thank you. I left my hat somewhere—just a bit too much sun, I think."

He let her go when she deliberately stepped back from him. They looked at each other. Rylee couldn't find the words to express how she felt, but she couldn't quite bring herself to walk away with nothing said.

"You came to the funeral," she finally whispered, breathlessly.

He nodded. "Aileen Jones was a good woman, an admirable horsewoman, so I came to pay my respects, despite our past differences. I hoped you would be there. I knew how much you loved her."

"I'm taking over the stables, and I intend to build it up into a reputable equestrian establishment."

Ash frowned. "And you don't want me tainting your reputation. Right?"

"I'm sorry, Ash, but there can never be anything between us. You destroyed our love the day you covered up the mistreatment of Arden's horses. No matter how I feel about you, I can't afford to be tainted by your reputation."

He reached out and gripped her forearms as he leaned closer. "You know it wasn't me, don't you? You know I was covering for Arden—a one-off mistake that could have killed her dream of riding in the Olympics."

A sudden rush of resentment stiffened her body. Ash let go of her.

"I know, but it doesn't matter. You publicly owned up to doing it. Mud sticks," she said.

"Rylee, please, I love you. Don't reject me like this."

His words seared through her. Her heart pumped hard, trying to keep the blood flowing through her frozen veins. Every inch of her lusted with need. The skin he touched felt alive and tingling. Her chest ached as she held down her sobs. She pulled away from him and almost sagged to the ground. With a herculean effort, she held herself upright. Her mouth was so dry she struggled to speak, tearing her tongue away from the roof of her mouth.

"We have no future, not while you willingly take the blame and continue to support Arden."

"For God's sake, Rylee, she's my baby sister. I have to support her."

"No you don't, not if she's doing wrong."

Ash swept his hat from his head and ran his hands through his hair. "But it was only once," he said.

"So you claim, but it's not true. Open your eyes. See what's going on. You have to choose—Arden or me."

He shook his head. "I can't."

"Then I'll choose for you, Ash." She immediately turned and walked away.

Staggered was probably a more apt description. She struggled to put one foot in front of the other, her chest clamped tight against gulping sobs and her throat dry and burning. She held herself together, but she couldn't stop the tears from escaping and rolling down her cheeks. As she struggled to find her way back to the car with blurred vision and her mind a mush of contradictory thoughts, she cursed the emotion that held her captive to Ash's spell. After reaching the car, she collapsed in the front seat before being overwhelmed by heaving sobs.

She was so engulfed in her misery she startled when the driver's door opened and her brother slid in beside her.

"So, you saw him then, sis?" Regan's voice sounded gentle and soothing.

She nodded.

"Shall we go home?" he asked.

She nodded again. Regan sighed as he started the car. They made the journey from the city in silence, but even as Rylee fought for control of her emotions, she sensed Regan's frustration and even disapproval.

* * * *

She'd waited tensely throughout the drive for him to chastise her, and he turned on her the moment they entered the house.

"For God's sake, Rylee, give up the stables if he means so much to you. Aileen would understand. I am sure she never meant you to suffer like this."

She stood there, letting his anger crash over her. He didn't understand and she didn't know how to make him. Without replying, she went into the kitchen to make a cup of tea.

Regan followed her. "I'm sorry for shouting, sis. But I can't bear seeing you in so much pain. All those years at home and still you grieve him."

She poured a cup of tea for both of them and handed Regan his before replying. "Regan, it isn't that simple. Even if I give up the stables and turn my back on Aunt Aileen's gift to me, I can't be with Ash. If we were together, it would be like condoning his actions, condoning Arden's cheating and cruelty. I can't tolerate cruelty to animals, so unless Ash declares himself innocent, I can't be with him, and he won't do that because Arden comes first. He won't clear himself because it will destroy her chances of competing in the Olympics, and he'll never do that, not even for me."

"Well then he's not worth it, sis."

She nodded. "I know, but I can't help how I feel. I don't know how to turn the feelings off."

Chapter Two

One thing Rylee could do was bury the troubling emotions deep, under a barrage of activity — in this case the rejuvenation of the stables. Together with Regan, she worked on the renovations — painting, re-roofing, putting up new fences and improving pastures. Every night she came inside so tired that she fell asleep the instant her head touched the pillow. When the worst of the renovations were done, they went out in search of suitable horses to supplement the six ponies and three horses Aileen had retained for general hacking and novice endurance riding — Monti, Zea and Lord Thornleigh, known affectionately as Thor, and of course dear old Shannon, Aileen's own horse.

While the underlying pining for Ash kept up a relentless throb, Rylee began to enjoy the work, providing lessons for beginners and trying out various eventing and endurance horses. She wanted a couple that would be suitable for beginners and a couple of higher quality mounts which would appeal to more experienced riders.

Attracting new clients was a slow, painful process and, as the days lengthened into weeks, she struggled with a growing sense of frustration and hopelessness as success seemed beyond her reach. When an opportunity came up to attend a workshop on marketing and business building by a renowned overseas guru, Rylee—urged on by Regan—decided to travel to Sydney to attend. She needed some direction on how to grow her business.

* * * *

The three-day business building conference was carefully balanced between work and networking with several opportunities for mingling. Rylee felt very out of her depth as she entered the function room for the first day meet-and-greet drinks, followed by dinner. She stood at the door and surveyed the crowd. A waiter flitted by, and she grabbed a glass of champagne, more for something to do than for the drink itself.

As she went to step into the throng, she saw Ash walking toward her. She clutched the stem of her champagne flute so tightly her hand trembled and she could barely breathe as she stood frozen to the spot. *What is he doing here?* He moved with the same familiar, lithe stride she remembered, his six-foot-three frame lean and supple. The dark charcoal suit hung from broad shoulders and his lavender shirt and matching striped tie accentuated his gorgeously toned body. Her heart jumped then beat in an uneven tattoo. No matter how strong her resolve was to stay immune to him, her body responded to his appearance with a tingling warmth that spread through her like wildfire. It had always been like that between them. No other man could elicit that sort of reaction without even touching her. He stopped about three feet away, as if waiting for a signal that would send him away or welcome him. She knew she should send him away, but she couldn't quite bring herself to do it.

He stepped closer. The tang of his aftershave enveloped her, invading her senses in a torturous pleasure of the familiar tangy spice she remembered. Her knees weakened, making it nigh on impossible to stand elegantly in her stilettos. She swallowed convulsively against a clamped throat, took a sip of champagne and let it slip down her throat to ease the tightness.

He examined her with an appraising stare. "You look stunning tonight."

"What the hell are you doing here?"

"I'm a last minute substitute for the keynote speaker. He had a heart attack."

"If I had known I wouldn't have come," she snapped, already backing away from him.

"Don't run away, please. Can we just talk?"

"We've talked already. There is nothing else to say."

"But there is. Where were you all those years, Rylee? No one could, or would, tell me where you'd run to. I couldn't find you, and I eventually gave up." His words were plaintive.

It put her on edge. "You were not meant to find me. It was better that way — for both of us."

"I don't believe that." He moved closer. "We were good together."

She stiffened at his nearness. "Maybe we were, but I still struggle to believe what I saw with my own eyes that day, Ash," she replied.

"It was ten years ago, surely water under the bridge," he said dismissively.

She shook her head, spikes of outrage sparking through her. "No, it's not. It never will be. I won't condone horse doping and I cannot come to terms with your support of Arden and her cruelties."

Dark resignation transformed his face, hardening the angles. "Rylee, it was just the one time. She's never done it again. She learned her lesson. Let it go, please."

"No. She has learned nothing. Neither have you, by the sound of it."

"Let it go. It doesn't matter anymore," he said soothingly.

His blasé attitude stung. "There can be nothing between us, not since that day. Not since you declared you doped that horse — lying, to protect Arden."

He lunged forward, grabbed her arms and hauled her into an all-encompassing embrace. She pushed against his muscular chest, overcome by a desperate need to be free of him. "Ash, let me go. Stop it. I don't want you mauling me. I value my reputation," she cried.

"Value, more than me?" His expression tightened into an unpleasant mask.

"Yes, Ash. The same way you value your lying sister and winning, more than me," she snapped back.

He guided her roughly out of the door and onto the balcony. She tried to resist, but failed against his superior strength. Short of screaming and making an exhibition of herself, she had little choice but to go with him. Without hesitation, he hauled her into the darkness of the private alcove and bent his head toward her. His mouth covered hers, commanding a response. The fire smoldering inside leaped into life and seared a fiery path from her belly to her brain. Instinctively she responded to the wave of raw lust that swept over her. She kissed him back with a hunger that was out of control. For a few short moments she lost herself in pure sexual need, drowning in the exquisite pleasure of his touch. Swamped by emotions long held in check, she was his, until a crash of glass inside brought the reality of the situation stabbing back at her and, with searing pain, she fought the hold of carnal desire. She pushed against his chest and tore her mouth from his, gasping for air—fresh air not tainted by the tantalizing aphrodisiac that was Ashford St. Clair.

"Stop it, Ash. I don't need this pain," she snapped and brought her hand up to slap him. Hot tears of shame welled in her eyes and rolled down her cheeks.

He caught her hand in his and wound it behind her back, forcing her against his chest. "Rylee, stop. It was all so long ago. For God's sake get over it."

She struggled against his hold. "Nothing has changed," she said. "The rumors are still rife about Arden's practices. I've heard them all and the equestrian world thinks you condone that. I cannot—will not—condone it."

"Am I ever going to live that down? For ten years I've borne the brunt of her mistake. Surely you had no doubts that it was Arden. So I was a fool to take the rap, but like you, she was only a kid. She wants so badly to ride in the Olympics."

Rylee shook her head. "She'll *never* represent Australia in the Olympics."

He gave her a little shake. "That's so judgmental. I never thought to hear you, of all people, say such things."

"Ash, you have to face facts. Your sister doesn't have the natural ability to win at such a high level. She's impatient with herself and her horses—down to the point of cruelty to get results."

"Damn you, Rylee. Who cares about Arden and her ambitions? I still love you, but it's obvious you no longer have feelings for me."

Rylee stared up at him, struggling to keep the tears from spilling onto her cheeks.

"Bullshit," she snapped. "You know there was never going to be anyone but you. I went back to my family. I needed time and distance. I hoped my heart would heal so I could move on. I thought I had until I saw you at the funeral. Despite everything, I still love you, but unless you publicly right the wrong from ten years ago, we have no future."

"I can't do that. You already know I will not destroy my sister's chances to be great. I have just got her two new horses—the best available. This year will be her year to shine. I can't take that from her, even if it means we can never be."

She shook her head. "You won't need to, Ash. She will do it for herself, but you can't see it—or won't see it. You're prepared to sacrifice what we could have to support a farce."

Ash pushed her away from him and stood stiffly in front of her. "I will not vilify my sister for one childish mistake."

Her arms hurt where he'd held her and she rubbed the flesh, determined to shrug down the pain of rejection. She glared up at him. "It's your choice, Ash. I hope it's not one you regret in the days that come."

She watched his contemptuous expression crumple into sadness before she retreated and walked back into the dining room. Her body ached with desire. Her heart clenched in regret for the one thing that kept them apart and her soul cried for the blind loyalty of the man she loved. She put her glass on the buffet table and turned away, only to find herself face to face with Arden.

"What are you doing here? Come to make more accusations? To turn the knife in his heart some more," the tall brunette said in an ominous tone.

"Arden," Rylee responded with artificial brightness.

Arden frowned, her beautiful red painted mouth curled up in a sneer. "He'll never take your accusations seriously — I can do no wrong in my big brother's eyes. Blood is thicker than water."

"Maybe he won't believe me, but that doesn't change anything — you are still abusing your horses,"

Arden gave a small snicker. "You can't prove a thing. Just like your godmother failed to prove anything on me ten years ago."

Rylee shook her head. "What about your brother? He had to stop competing because he took the rap for you. Now he has a permanent black mark against his name. Doesn't that worry you? He always had a better chance to win than you."

"It was his choice," Arden muttered. She looked down.

"You betrayed us both that day. I can't forgive you," Rylee shouted.

"Huh! I don't care what you think, Rylee. My brother still loves me and I'm still competing. Too bad it's too late for you and him. Go back under the rock you crawled out from, Rylee O'Shaughnessy," Arden sneered.

"Damn you, Arden. You will be found out — one day," Rylee threatened, even though deep down she doubted it would happen.

Suddenly, the noise surrounding her became unbearable and her close proximity to Ash's conniving sister and her ex best friend made her feel sick. She pushed past Arden and hurried from the room. She needed to be far away from the woman who had ruined her life.

The lift pinged when it arrived and she stepped inside, but before the doors could close, Ash inserted his body in the opening. Her heart jumped and her body tingled with the force of his masculine presence in the enclosed space of the lift. The chemistry of his nearness, his smell and untamed masculinity teased her with its sexy tang. *I want this man so badly. To hold him, to love him and to make passionate love with him.* No matter his flaws in regards to his sibling, she still loved him. Could she cross the line, knowing they had no future? It went against the strong morality of her Catholic upbringing, but the desire throbbing through her body needed to be satisfied. How she would heal the emptiness in her heart she had no idea. Maybe she never would.

He swept her into his embrace. "If you can give me no more, Rylee, spend the night with me, please. We have both waited so long for this. I want to make love to you." His words were indistinct, muffled against her skin where he nuzzled against her neck.

She shook her head and tried to extract herself from his hold. "Ash…it will make the situation worse… I spoke to Arden."

"Damn my sister. Forget her for the moment. This is about *us*."

"No, Ash. It can never be just about how we feel. Arden stands between us and she's not about to give up her misguided ambitions for us. She has too much to lose."

His mouth smothered her anguished protest. She let herself respond to the fiery demand of his kiss, reveling in the taste of him. When she parted her lips a little, he immediately took advantage of her moment of weakness. He wrapped his tongue around hers, sucking gently. She trembled with desire, a burning desire, sparked by the very taste of him. Her knees softened under his onslaught and the passion ignited in her belly. He held her crushed against the hardness of his chest. She could feel his erection pressing into her lower abdomen. Tremors shook her. To be held by him after so long with only her memories and her dreams to remember his touch, his scent, his taste and his unbridled sensuousness... She yearned with a desperate need to be possessed by him. To have his cock buried deep inside her in a lusty joining that would wipe the intervening years into oblivion. Suddenly all the reasons and excuses for why they couldn't be together melted into a puddle of arousal. She grabbed his butt and pulled him closer. Right now she didn't care if they were together one night or one year or eternity. She desperately wanted him, and be damned to the opinions of others.

To make her invitation clear, she reached up and wrapped her arms around his neck. "Take me to bed, Ash."

Ash lifted her into his arms and pushed his way through the door of the lift before striding down the corridor and into his room. The door had barely shut behind them and he attacked her zip. He slid it down and unclipped her bra. Rylee wiggled a little and her classy little black dress and brief lacy knickers were in a pile at her feet. With his mouth still glued to hers, he lifted her again and walked her to the bed. She fell backward, landing with a small bounce on the soft bed, her legs dangling over the side. Ash stood between her knees and shed his shirt and jacket, chucking them with a flick of his wrist onto the chair in the corner. She watched him undo his belt. With long slim fingers he leisurely undid his fly. He stared directly into her eyes. With seductive slowness he pushed his pants and trunks down over his hips. His cock leaped up, stiff and throbbing, as it escaped the confines of the material. His hairless groin was surprisingly sensual, his balls a rosy pink hanging between his muscular thighs. She could see the veins pulsing in the thick length.

He knelt between her legs, lifted her feet and placed them on the bed. The action bent her knees and exposed her to his eager perusal. He shuffled forward on his knees and kissed her inner thighs, one side then the other, moving steadily closer to where her throbbing nub was hidden by the soft curve of her mound. He flicked his tongue across her flesh, inch by inch closer. She moaned. Her pussy tightened with need and she could feel her juices dribble out of her. Ecstasy almost overwhelmed her when he reached the little hood hiding the erect flesh of her clit and searched under it with his tongue. With her most sensitive spot exposed to his ministrations he sucked on it drawing it out with tender little strokes. Her legs trembled under the blistering passion that rolled over her like molten lava, the main eruption building toward a fiery explosion. He lifted himself upright and she wriggled a little farther on the bed. He lowered himself over her, his cock just resting in the center of her lips, as if waiting for her encouragement before sinking into her.

"Oh God, I want you, Rylee," he murmured.

She reached down and took his penis in her grasp, urged him to plunge into her. At her encouragement, he pressed downward and penetrated deep inside.

She almost screamed with pleasure as his erection filled and stretched her. Instinctively she wrapped her legs around his hips and gripped him close. He thrust, deep and fast. She struggled to breathe. Her body tensed and shook in the build up to her climax. He took her mouth with his, immediately demanding access. He probed deeply and she in turn sucked on his tongue, feeling its moist and slightly rough surface against hers. His taste was intoxicating. His scent wafted around her and she smelled the tangy bouquet of sex as their bodies bucked and pressed together and the fluid of their shared arousal spread on their bodies. She loved the feel of his smooth groin rubbing on her and wondered what it would feel like if they were both shaved.

He moaned and sweat trickled down his chest. She grabbed his shoulders and ran her nails down his back until she cupped his buttocks and urged him to pump harder and deeper. He grunted with the force that brought their bodies slamming together. She screamed then—the feel of his head rubbing her cervix igniting the last wave of her arousal into an explosion. Her climax gathered—a tsunami ready to crash over her. He thrust faster and deeper. Her body shuddered and jerked under his assault, the force of her climax bulldozing through her body, sweeping consciousness and reason before it. She gasped and for a moment—a split second—she lost touch with reality. Every nerve in her body danced and her muscles clenched and relaxed around his hot flesh. Under the onslaught of her own release, she barely appreciated his release pulsing down the length of his shaft and squirting hot cum into her. She sagged onto the bed. He stilled, spent. She tightened her pussy muscles as he softened, making him groan. They lay still for quite a while, and

Rylee was acutely aware of Ash struggling to gain control of his breathing. Tears welled in her eyes and a sob gripped her chest. Ten years she had waited to consummate her love and it overwhelmed her now the act was completed. An incredible feeling of warmth and contentment flowed over her with the small shuddering aftershocks that rippled through her body. He rolled off her, pulling her tight against him. She peeked up into his face and saw wetness in his eyes. He brought his head down and gently nibbled at her bottom lip and placed featherlight kisses all around her mouth.

"All those wasted years, Rylee. We were meant for each other."

Rylee sighed in response to the cloud of reality that had weaseled its way back into her mind. "Maybe, Ash, but it can't be unless you violate your commitment to Arden."

"But what can be wrong with something that feels so heavenly—that feels so right," he protested as he snuggled closer. "We can work things out, Rylee. I'm so glad you're back. Will you stay with me tonight? I know we both have an early session in the morning, but I just want to hold you."

* * * *

When she woke the next morning, Ash still held her. The alarm hadn't gone off, but Rylee slipped from his bed and dressed. She kissed him, and he stirred. "See you later," she whispered.

"Tonight—dinner," he mumbled, barely opening his eyes.

She smiled inside and out, all day, keeping her mind one step ahead of the shadow of reality. The session on marketing and business management was interesting and very informative. To make the stables a financial success, she needed to bring it into the twenty-first century. She saw Ash as she moved between sessions, and he waved and grinned as he passed.

* * * *

She had just finished dressing when he knocked on the door. He grabbed her, whirled her around the room then kissed her commandingly. She sank under his hungry onslaught until they parted breathlessly.

"Let's skip dinner," he suggested, eying her king-size bed.

She laughed. "You can't, Ash. The participants expect you to show."

He smiled now. "I know. Are you ready?"

She nodded and preceded him out of the door. They were seated at a table of six. Fortunately Arden was not one of them. Nevertheless, Rylee could feel her poisonous stare burning between her shoulder blades from across the room. She wondered if Arden knew that her precious brother had spent the night with her—and if she did, whether it made her feel threatened.

Everyone, including Rylee, was excited about what they had learned and they exchanged ideas and brainstormed right through the entrée and main course. As they ate dessert, each participant helped collate ideas and talk them through with Ash. When most of the people had drifted away either into the bar or upstairs, Ash handed her his room key. "Go on up. I just have to check the lecture room for tomorrow. I'll be up soon."

"Ash." Arden's strident cry froze them both into tense expectation.

Ash turned to face his sister, the expression on his face less than welcoming. "Arden?"

Rylee flinched at the toxic expression on Arden's face.

"How can you, Ash? She betrayed you and is determined to destroy my business ambitions. She is so righteous that she would betray both of us right now if she thought we were hurting the horses. How can you betray me like this?" she cried. Her expression was almost tragic, except for the sharp edge of malice.

Ash stared at his sister. "Rylee had nothing to do with my downfall. Aileen Jones saw me with the stuff, Arden. Whether I administered it or not is irrelevant."

Arden scowled. "Her or the old woman, it's one and the same. They're both guilty of wanting me eliminated." She pointed at Rylee. "She just wanted to win—to win on that rag tag nag she used to ride, one she knew would never come up to my animals. The pair of them had to find a way to bring me down. We were friends. You don't betray your friends."

"For God's sake, Arden. I've never heard such rubbish. Winning wasn't my goal, unlike you. You did wrong. How could I pretend, when your horse collapsed, that it was okay? Ignore the fact that you had been doing unethical things to gain an advantage over us all. Including me, your best friend?"

"Bullshit. You were never going to win any other way than to eliminate me, not on that old dobbin you had. No, your godmother had to destroy Ash and eliminate me to ensure you won. It was a real coup for you. And the business thrived after that, at least for a while—after she lied and kicked me out."

"She didn't lie, and you know it," Rylee declared.

"Enough you two," Ash shouted. "The horse *was* doped by you, Arden. I took the rap and you still have your opportunities, so leave Rylee out of it."

Arden stood straight and tall, then looked directly at her brother—her expression a bitter twisted mask of hatred. "So you're going to take her side now. Abandon me. You know she'll never let you forget you're a horse doper, brother dear. Never."

"Oh shut up. I'll never abandon you. I can have both..."

"No, you can't," Rylee yelled at them.

"See? The high and mighty Rylee O'Shaughnessy doesn't want to be tarnished with the same brush as us 'horse dopers'," Arden screeched.

"Enough!" Ash yelled.

"No, not enough. Rylee, get out of my face and keep your grasping little Irish hands off my brother. We don't need your judgmental attitude. Besides, you're not even competing anymore, so what can it matter to you what I—we—do?" Arden sneered.

Rylee slammed her clenched fists onto her hips and glared at her foe. "It does matter. Honesty, integrity and the best treatment for horses matter. Will always matter."

"Enough, you two," Ash snapped.

Arden glared at her brother then turned to Rylee. "You can give him your body and he'll take it, but he'll never put you first. His family—me, his baby sister—will always be his priority."

"Arden..." Ash protested half-heartedly.

Arden pointed at Rylee. "Huh, I can see it on your face. You've already sacrificed your virtue in an effort to win him away from me. More fool you." Arden laughed—a high pitched sniggering sound that ended in a series of snorts.

Barely able to keep her temper in check, Rylee glared from Arden to Ash then turned on her heel and stalked away, the card to his room still in her hand.

Chapter Three

The shudders assailing her body were so violent Rylee could barely walk straight in her heels. Nausea washed over her and every nerve ending to the roots of her hair sizzled with fury. No repentance, not an ounce of repentance. And was Arden right? Had she been trying to lure Ash from his sister's clutches by sleeping with him? For a moment she regretted her actions, feeling as if she had somehow sold herself. *But damn it was good to finally feel his cock thrust into me. All I had until last night was dreams. The sex had been worth waiting for and I will not feel any shame at giving my body to Ash.*

A chill ran over her skin as she leaned on the door of her room and slashed the key card through the lock. The door swung open and Rylee staggered forward with it. Damn Arden and damn Ash and damn her own gullible weakness.

In an effort to center herself, Rylee poured a glass of wine, slipped into her nightie and sat at the small desk. She used some sheets of hotel lecture pad to outline her plans for the stables, including what she could offer, a point of difference and how to get her message out to the public. By the time she had filled the third page with ideas, the trembling had eased and she felt calmer. She didn't regret having sex with Ash, and it did not damage her plans for the future—just eased an unsatisfied ache from the past.

Rylee was well into the basic outline of her marketing plan when there was a tap on the door.

"Rylee, please open the door?" he asked.

He pushed into the room the moment she opened the door.

"I've been waiting for you." She held out his card. "You've come for this," she said.

"No. I've come for you," he replied.

"Arden isn't going to approve."

"Forget Arden. I don't have to ask permission from my sister as to whom I bed. This is between us."

He came up behind her and grasped her shoulders. She wanted Ash. She couldn't lie to herself or him. Despite the ugly scene downstairs, she still loved this man, but she silently cursed herself for how she had melted when he'd nuzzled her neck and shoulders, and her pussy became a puddle of molten desire.

"I have waited all day for this, Ry. Last night wasn't enough. I don't think I'll ever get enough of you." He continued to kiss her neck and cheeks, then he caressed her cleavage before moving inside her bra to cup her breasts.

Despite the tight fit for his large hand, he managed with a tender touch to tease her nipples erect. She reached between them and massaged the solid ridge of his erection through his pants. Ash ran his fingers through her hair, massaging the scalp. Her whole head tingled with the soothing, but stimulating, pressure of the circular movement. She tipped her head forward to allow him to stroke down the back of her neck and across her shoulders. She almost purred under his ministrations. He took her hands and guided them up the inside of her thighs until they connected with the flimsy lace of her G-string. He pushed the panties aside and using Rylee's fingers, he dipped into her and delicate circles spread her fluids around. Rylee stroked her own flesh and teased her clit. He slipped the straps off her shoulders and tugged the nightie and bra down to her waist. Now he cupped her breasts and teased the nipples before lifting her off the chair. Her outer clothes dropped to the floor then she wriggled out of her panties. Ash shed his clothes with hurried movements, releasing his already hard cock to stand straight out from his groin. She enclosed his heated flesh with her palms and stroked up and down the shaft, skimming right over his head, administering a firm squeeze. He sat and pulled her onto his lap, facing him. Rylee sat on his thighs, her legs spread wide. He reached under her and explored the folds of her intimate flesh. He pulled her a little closer. His swollen rod poked up between their bodies, the tight dark pink skin of his head glistening with pre-cum. He teased her clit, running a finger and thumb around the base and over the tip. Then he boosted her upwards and she wriggled forward until poised over his throbbing cock. Ash semi-supported her so she could lower herself onto him, just enough so the tip of his penis pushed into her pussy, bringing an incredible need for penetration. Rylee so wanted to let the full length of his hardness sink into her for his shallow dips were maddening and erotic. She wanted satisfaction.

"Damn it, Ash. Stop playing and just fuck me. I can't stand it anymore," she cried.

He chuckled and dipped in again and again. Her pussy clenched at his stiff shaft, trying to pull it in before he took it away. She almost screamed with need when with a decisive stroke he lowered her and plunged his whole length to the hilt inside her. They moved in unison. Each lift pulled his cock right out of her body, only to be thrust in again on the downward movement so deep it stretched her opening, sending pulses of exquisite sensation barreling through her.

He kissed her breasts, sucking at her erect nipples and smothering her chest and neck with light kisses and gentle nibbles. He ran his tongue around her earlobes and dipped his tongue into them. She moaned. He skimmed the skin with his hands from her waist down over her hips and to her buttocks. He cupped them angling her slightly forward, so he pressed more against the back wall of her pussy. She moaned again. He thrust faster, and she met his increased rhythm. Her body throbbed and her legs trembled, but all that mattered was the feel of his cock pushing its way into her, stretching her hot flesh. She clenched her muscles and bounced up and down. Her climax built, aching in her hips with an almost unbearable throb. He reached under her and caressed her clit. The touch of his fingertip ignited a fiery blaze that flared and sparked until she exploded with mind-numbing force. Rylee clawed at his shoulders and bore down on his cock as he stroked the tip of her sensitive nub with rapid little flicks and sank into her, deep and fast. Her body convulsed with wave after wave of sensation that rolled through her. She gripped his shoulders and leaned forward. Her whole body spasmed. Tiny moans escaped under the force of her release. The intense undulations slowed and Ash changed tempo, giving fast shallow pokes before he pushed hard into her and stilled. She collapsed onto his lap and rested her head on his shoulder. He embraced her and they rocked gently on the chair, soaking up the last miniscule waves of sensations where their bodies were joined. Their sweat mingled and their breathing gradually slowed to normal. A sudden chill brushed her naked body.

She moved slightly. "Ash, I'm getting cold," she murmured.

"Mmmmm." He circled her waist and stood, pulling his cock out of her with the movement, even though she tried to hold onto it. With reverent care he set her down on the crisp white sheets then climbed in beside her.

They lay on their backs side by side, just touching along the full length of their bodies. He entwined his fingers through hers.

"It seems only like yesterday that we parted. Ten long years wasted, Rylee. We should have made love then, even though you were too young. You never would have left if we had. Did you think of me when you were gone?"

"Oh, Ash, I tried not to think of you. I went home to forget you. To stop loving you."

"But you didn't," he said.

"No, I didn't."

He rolled toward her laying one arm over waist. "I'm glad you didn't.

* * * *

He was watching her when she woke sometime just after dawn. She reached up and stroked his cheek feeling the slight abrasiveness of new beard growth. His expression was pensive.

"What are you thinking, Ash?"

"Why didn't you come back, after everything died down—I mean, if you still loved me?"

"Because, unless you owned up to lying for Arden, there could never be anything between us. I tried to forget you, but I couldn't even though my family tried everything to help me—most of my siblings and my stepmother."

"You have a stepmother?"

"Yes, a wonderful woman. She took us all on and added three more to the brood. It relieved me of being a substitute mother for everyone. She gave me back my life. She has so much love and such generosity. We gave her so much hell in the beginning that it's a wonder she didn't flee in the night or go mad. It is a task I would never want to take on."

"Would it be so bad to mother the child of the man you loved?"

She shook her head. "But you don't have a child—do you?"

"Actually I do. A daughter, Lillian, but we all call her Lilli."

Rylee sat right up and glowered down at him, the beginnings of anger roiling in her stomach. "And just when did you plan on telling me you have a daughter?"

He shrugged. "I don't know... When it came up, I suppose."

"When it came up!" Rylee cried.

"Rylee," he soothed.

"Are you also saying you're married?"

"No, Rylee. I wouldn't do that to you. I'm a widower. My wife Julie died just after Lillian was born. She went riding on one of Arden's horses. It bolted, bucked and threw her off. She broke her neck."

"You allowed her to ride one of Arden's horses? What were you thinking? Those horses are so damaged and confused by Arden's training methods I'm surprised Arden isn't dead yet. That is so awful. So tragic for you. I am so sorry you've had so much pain."

"So you're saying this is my fault too." Ash sat up.

"No—it's Arden's fault,"

"You want to make everything Arden's fault," Ash accused, as a deep frown settled on his forehead. "Why do you hate her so much?"

"I would hate anyone doing wrong by their horses and forcing their family to take the blame," Rylee replied. "But it's not that. I hate her because she destroyed what we had. You let her. You let your sister obliterate our love through her evil doing. We can never get that back."

"Why? Because I have two strikes against my name now—being a horse doper and being careless because I let my wife die? Damn it."

"It's got nothing to do with your wife. It's to do with loyalty to me. You vowed you loved me. Yet you chose your sister. You put her first, damn you."

"Yes, I did, but it never changed how I felt about you. I want you in my life. We need to get past this, but I don't know how."

"We can't."

"Blast it all, Rylee."

"You have two loyalties now, your sister and your daughter. I can't compete with Arden—that I already know—and I won't compete with your child."

"But you have no need to compete with anyone. Arden is her own person, and my daughter is but a child and I have no desire for you to become a stepmother for her. She's at boarding school, so you'll have me for most of the time. I'll be a devoted, faithful lover. We will have a good life together."

"You bastard, Ashford St. Clair. Maybe I don't want to just be your bit on the side. Maybe I want marriage, security, love. Maybe I want children of my own. Have you thought that through? What if I get pregnant? What would become of 'our' child?"

His face paled then. "You wouldn't do that, would you? You always said you didn't want to be a mother. That you didn't want kids."

"Ten years ago I was seventeen, a child. Things change. I grew up."

"You were so adamant. I... I was sure you wouldn't want children of your own. That you would be happy to..." His voice faded into silence.

"You're a bastard. Just thinking of *you*. Always you... No, I won't get pregnant, but I am not prepared to live some sort of half-life with you. Besides, you're deliberately ignoring the horse doping."

"You keep harping on about it. It was a one-time mistake on her part. Without my support she won't make it to the top level. I can't withdraw my support." He said it slowly, as if he was spelling it out for her — or himself.

"But you're supporting her in wrongdoing," Rylee cried.

"I don't believe the rumors. She promised she would never ever do anything like that again and I must believe her. Besides, if she was doing wrong, she would have been caught by now. No, it is nothing but vicious rumors," he stated firmly.

"Then you are a fool. A bloody, blind fool." She rolled out of bed and dragged the sheet around her still-glowing body. "Unless you open your eyes and see what's right under your nose, there can be nothing more between us. I won't risk my reputation or my business because of your blind loyalty to your sister. Get out of my room. Leave me alone."

He made no move to concede as he pulled on his clothes and left, leaving her bitterly disappointed. Like a fool, she had hoped that the loving they had shared would have meant something to him, perhaps enough to reconsider his position. Not that she regretted having sex with him. When he had gone, she let the tears well up and fall down her cheeks, feeling so betrayed and humiliated. She shouldn't have assumed because he had wanted her body so badly that they would ultimately have a life together. She should have known better. But even that only hurt a little, in comparison to his unexpected assertion he did not want her to be stepmother to his daughter. She wondered if someone had said something to him—if someone close to her had revealed her terrible secret that she was irresponsible when it came to children. It cut deep into her own well-hidden insecurities. She didn't exactly have a good track record. One word with her father and Ash would be left in no doubt she was irresponsible. Rohan should never have died under her care.

The past continued to haunt her and her father made sure she never forgot it. She had been substitute mother to her eleven siblings when her mother had died in childbirth. It had been a struggle, the mothering. She had made mistakes, got tired, grumpy and resentful of the sacrifice asked of her. She had fought with her father day in and day out about his expectations and the brutal discipline he often dished out to both sons and daughters. One day after she had been up most of the night with the youngest, she had gotten the older ones off to school and thinking the two littlies were safe with the door shut, she had nodded off at the kitchen table. She had been woken by little Adana screaming hysterically. She had lifted her up and prepared a bottle, but it was only when the child had finally settled that she'd realized young Rohan was nowhere to be found. She'd searched the house, the sheds, the stables and yards, worried, but as it had begun to get dark, she'd panicked. With Adana on her hip, she'd run to find Mrs. Binchey in the next cottage. Her sons had been home already and within half an hour, a full search had been under way for the four year old. Her father had already known Rohan was missing before he'd reached the cottage, raging through the door in a furious temper. He'd grabbed her collar and dragged her inside to the pantry. Here he'd ripped her skirt up over her head bent her over the nearest chair and thrashed her with the wide leather belt that held his trousers up.

"You careless, lazy, little bitch. Can't even trust you to watch a tiny tot barely steady on his feet. You just let him walk out the door damn it?" he'd bellowed and with each word he'd hit.

The pain had cut through her as the strap had laid welts and bloody lines in its path, cutting her knickers to ribbons and exposing her backside to the sharp edge of the leather. Her father had ignored her screams. On and on he'd gone. Rylee had shut much of the hateful tirade out. Consumed with guilt, Rylee was sure her father would have beaten her to death if the searchers had not returned so soon with the child's limp body draped in a rug. Rohan, his youngest son, dead and it was her fault.

He had never forgiven her. She had lived in the house, but no longer considered it her home. She had cared for the people she lived with, but she could no longer regard them as family. Rylee's aunt, her mother's sister Mary, had been her salvation and sanity, but no matter how much she pleaded with her brother-in-law, Fagan O'Shaughnessy had never softened his stance toward Rylee. He made it clear he would never forgive her for the carelessness that robbed him of his youngest son. To this day, she remained unforgiven by him and herself.

She also knew about stepmothers. Hers had come on the scene some six years after her mother's death and she had stepped in and mothered her new husband's brood with love, humor and fairness. That fairness had remained even when she'd had three of her own, all boys. She'd advocated for Rylee, but her father would not be swayed, even though he now had five strapping sons. Rylee loved and admired her father's second wife and didn't believe for a moment she could even come near this amazing woman's ability to love another women's children.

She hugged her perceived failures with her siblings close to her soul, each one huge in her memory and coated in guilt. Even though they didn't hold it against her, she held it against herself. Roisin—a year older than Rohan and inseparable from her younger brother—agreed with their father's stance as soon as she'd been old enough to understand and they hadn't spoken civilly for years. It had been a huge burden for Rylee while she had hidden in Tassie. Being ostracized by her father and sister perpetuated her punishment and added to the tremendous burden of guilt she continued to carry inside at her failure to keep her brother safe. She never trusted herself again with the supervision of any children, but those she might have of her own, and even then she wasn't sure she deserved to be a mother.

The thought of being responsible for Ash's child terrified her, but that didn't mean she could withstand the insult and hurt Ash had inflicted by making it clear she was not a suitable stepmother for his child.

* * * *

The next morning she skipped the farewell breakfast—too vulnerable and too angry to face Ash right now. Suddenly the future appeared tarnished, there would be no romantic re-union with Ash and all she had left was the stables, and she wasn't sure if this was enough. She'd dated in Tassie, but never found anyone that could ignite a spark in her heart. Now she knew that her heart wasn't dead, as she had often suspected, but in cold storage for Ashford St. Clair. He was her one true soulmate and the handsome prince who could awaken the sleeping beauty.

Chapter Four

When the door opened, Ash looked up, expecting Rylee. He hoped that she had thought over his proposal and decided it would work for them. He had just a fleeting second to feel disappointed when he saw Arden before she charged across the room and slapped him about the head and shoulders.

"So, have you got her out of your system now, big brother? A couple nights of hot sex should have soothed the itch." She thumped him again and again with her clenched fists.

He struggled from under her attack and moved to the other side of the bed. "Don't be so disgusting, Arden. I just happen to love Rylee—regardless of the angst between you two."

"You're a fool, Ash," Arden shouted. "She's no good for you. What about Lilli? You know Rylee is hopeless with kids. Can't stand them. She would run a mile before she took on the stepmother role."

Ash stood straighter, his fists clenched at his sides. "She never said she couldn't stand kids."

"All I heard when we were riding together was how much she resented giving up her life to be a substitute mother to all her eleven siblings. She doesn't even want kids of her own. Too much like slavery, she used to say," Arden sniped in a childlike voice.

"Arden, seventeen year olds say things like that all the time. It doesn't mean Rylee thinks that way today."

"Huh. Did you tell her you had a daughter?"

"I did. I also told her, clearly, I didn't need a stepmother for Lilli."

Arden frowned. "And how did she take it?"

"Well, she didn't seem happy and sent me packing."

Arden slapped her hands on her hips and tilted her head to the side. "See? I told you so. She will use the horses to excuse herself. She would never tell you she didn't like kids. Then what would happen to Lilli if you marry her? Poor Lilli—you don't want her to suffer like I did. Resented, every day. Tortured or ignored. Would you put Lilli through that?"

Ash looked away for a moment. No, he would not put Lilli at risk of a nasty stepmother. Not that he could reconcile in his head the Rylee he knew and anything nasty. His aching need for Rylee was a constant mental and physical torment and the thought that she would not want to mother his daughter enhanced it, but Ash knew he would always put his daughter first.

"Besides, Lilli does not need anyone else. She has me," Arden crowed.

Ash contemplated his sister. She wasn't boasting, for Lilli idolized Arden. They did lots of mother-daughter things during the holidays, especially when Ash went away for work. The one thing that faded the rosy picture was Ash's edict that Lilli did not ride and

Arden's resentment of his decision. Even though his marriage to his late wife Julie had been disappointing for both of them after the first surge of lust was exhausted he had been traumatized by her fatal horse riding accident and now feared for his beloved daughter's safety around Arden's horses. Not that the question came up often because Lilli boarded at St Wilhelmina's School.

"I know Lilli has you, but I want Rylee."

"Well, sometimes we can't have what we want, big brother."

"Damn it. I have kept your secret and supported you for ten years. I want the woman I love."

"And you would destroy my future? Would you really? For some trumped up little affair and hot sex. I would *never* forgive you."

Ash sighed. "No, I won't do anything to destroy your future, but I'll have to convince Rylee to forgive me."

"Forgive, ha! Give it up, brother."

Ash glared at his sister. "Bugger off and leave me to wallow, okay? Go play with your precious horses."

Arden stormed out of the room, slamming the door behind her.

Ash sank back on the bed and stared at the ceiling. His chances of a satisfactory solution to his relationship with Rylee were shrinking by the minute. Arden, Rylee and Lilli, the three people he loved — God damn it, how the hell he could reconcile this conflict was tearing him to pieces.

He knew he would have to talk to Rylee — seriously — about Lilli, Arden and their future — if they had a future. She had made it clear she wouldn't just be his part-time partner, and he thought he'd detected a desire for her own children. He was glad he had to go away for a couple of weeks. It would give him some head space to decide just what he wanted and how much he was prepared to compromise to work things out with Rylee. Despite Arden's cynicism, he was determined not to let Rylee slip from his life. He loved her. If he didn't they were going to shred his heart and his sanity.

Arden had made great progress in the last few years and hoped to be chosen for the Olympic team if she completed the requirements for qualification. He couldn't betray her as Rylee suggested, but he had no idea how to get her to accept his past actions when he had trouble accepting the connotations that came with his lie to save his sister's future. He missed competing but there was nothing that would lure him back into eventing to face the gossips and innuendo that would undoubtedly fly around.

And as for Lilli, he was confused. He thought by relieving Rylee of any real responsibility for his child, she would have been pleased, but instead she was furious and claimed to want her own children. Things had definitely changed in the ten years apart. It was complicated and he was perplexed and disorientated about the next move, scared stiff he would destroy everything.

* * * *

Rylee breathed in deeply as she stepped out of the taxi. The fresh cold air was overlain with the rustic earthy smells of wood smoke, horse, leather and hay to welcome her home.

Regan appeared at the stable door. "Good to have you home, sis. Come here. We have an addition to the family."

She left her case and followed him into the warm, dim interior. In the third loose box stood her new mare, Sapphire Cloud. At her side, nuzzling at her teat, stood a dark gray foal—a filly.

She leaned on the gate and stared at the baby. "Oh, Regan, she's so beautiful. I gather everything went well."

"It did. So how was the conference?"

She stared at the horses, unable to face her brother's scrutiny.

"Sis?" Regan urged

"Ashford St. Clair was there," she said dully.

"And...?"

She shrugged. "Nothing's changed."

"You still love him then? We all know you have never stopped loving him all these years."

She looked up at her brother. "No, I have never stopped loving him and apparently he still loves me, but nothing's changed. His sister is to remain innocent while he continues to carry the rap for her."

Now the tears welled up and rolled down her cheeks. "Oh, Regan, I've made such an idiot of myself."

Regan took her into his embrace. "You slept with him then?" he asked softly.

She nodded against his shoulder. "I love him."

"Never mind. Maybe he just needs to think it through."

"No he's never going to betray his sister. Now he has a daughter and he made it clear he does not want me to mother his child. Someone must have told him about Rohan. So where does it leave me?" she asked.

"I don't know, sis, but surely he can't hold that against you?"

She shrugged. "Why not? My father does."

"Yeah, but our father is different. He's a hard man."

"He's a parent. So is Ash," she replied, as she left the stable and went to unpack. *So you've done it now. You know what it's like to be loved by Ash. Now get on with it, woman. Make these stables great. It's all you've got.* She felt the sting of tears in her eyes, but she blinked them back. There was no use crying. Maybe when he had time to think it through, to realize how much they meant to each other, he would change his mind.

* * * *

The days passed slowly. The phone hung heavy in the pocket of her workpants as Rylee mucked out, cleaned tack and prepared feeds. She expected him to call. Surely he would call. Her mind refused to process his proposal that she become his mistress. The idea scored painful slices across her heart and her pride. She had expected a complete retraction—if not immediately, by now. As each day passed and it didn't come, Rylee began to slide into melancholy and she suspected this is how he intended to end their relationship. A great love ending with a brooding silence.

Regan tried to jolly her out of her mood and for his sake, she tried to appear upbeat, but it was when she worked alone in the stables with only the horses for company that she allowed herself to indulge in a little self-pity. And horses were great listeners. Rylee had no regrets about consummating her love, but she wished she had gone into the situation with a more realistic view of the outcome. He hadn't put her first ten years ago and with Arden on the verge of qualifying for selection on the Olympic team, why would he change his decision now?

* * * *

The next two weeks were madly busy. Some of Rylee's marketing strategies came to fruition quite quickly with two schools coming in for a heavily discounted five-lesson course held over a week. Rylee loved having the groups in. Teaching them about horses, how to care for them, how to ride and be safe and how to love them. She had no concerns about these kids because they had two eagle-eyed teachers supervising them and Regan by her side.

She had secured new customers from these groups, where the child leased a horse and took total responsibility for it on the proviso that an adult was there to supervise each time. Sometimes the parents bought them a horse and stabled it with Rylee.

This was where Rylee intended to expand — with more stables and a second undercover riding arena. She had the money to achieve it with what her godmother Aileen had left her, in addition to the stables set on twenty acres of land. She had discussed the plans with her godmother before she'd passed away. It was really her dream, but she had got too old and too sick to achieve it. Rylee now had the chance to realize Aileen's dream and her own, especially now that Regan had joined her. She did wish she had enough money to buy the place next door. She would have loved to set up a cross-country course and allow for endurance ride training and a stud. She had big dreams but to secure them, she had to keep away from Ash lest his reputation damage hers. She already knew that one could live with a broken heart and function adequately.

* * * *

The fire crackled merrily, making the room warm and cozy as Rylee sat across the desk from her brother, discussing the current financial position of the stables and how they could best afford the expansion. Rylee pulled out her notes from the conference and together they drew up a business plan. Rylee made some tentative projections, knowing full well she had to get more of her clients to enter into the horse shows, endurance rides and other events to raise the profile of her stables in the equestrian world. She had convinced two of her older clients to enter the junior section of a limited distance endurance ride through Kypo forest on the weekend. They had been training for weeks. The horses were fit and the girls, more than capable.

The phone's shrill ring shattered their quiet communication.

"Rylee," she said absently, still watching her brother doing calculations.

"It's Ash. Please don't hang up."

"What do you want?" Her tone was brusque.

"We need to talk. It can't end like this. I need you."

"I don't think there is anything to talk about. You made your stance pretty clear on just how much you *need* me," she grumbled.

"Please, just have dinner with me. I'm sure we can work this out."

"No, I don't think so," she replied.

She saw her brother shaking his head. "Go, Rylee. Give him a chance to redeem himself."

"Sorry. Am I interrupting you?" Ash asked.

Rylee adjusted the phone, puzzled at her brother's urging. "No, it was just my brother. For some strange reason, he appears to be on your side. So when do you want to have dinner?"

"Tomorrow night," Ash suggested.

"Fine. I'll meet you at Il Palatino at seven," Rylee agreed.

"I could come and pick you up," Ash offered.

"No. I'll see you tomorrow night. Goodbye." She disconnected and flopped back in her chair. "Good grief, Regan, now what have I done? Why the hell did you suggest I go?"

"The right thing. You love him. Take a chance, sis. Maybe you can have both."

For the next twenty-four hours she fretted and questioned her decision. Here she was walking right into a storm of heart ache, but somehow it didn't feel finished. Something more needed to be said.

* * * *

Ash was seated outside. He watched her walk across the road to the restaurant. There was hunger in his expression and tiredness around his eyes. So he'd missed her just as much as she had missed him these last couple of weeks. Her sympathy store was a little on the low side. He smiled as she arrived at the table, stood and pulled out her chair. He made no attempt to kiss her.

With their order taken, Ash took her hand in his. "I'm sorry, Rylee. I didn't mean to hurt you."

"Oh, I am sure you didn't," she responded with a sharp edge of sarcasm, fully expecting this conversation to lead to more emotional hurt.

He shrugged. "But I did and I'm sorry. What I offered was demeaning and based on outdated assumptions. I should have asked you, talked it through with you, but... Well, I wanted to make love to you so badly that I didn't think. But the thing is, Rylee... It's not just me now." He stilled and stared up at her, his expression full of guilt. "Lillian is eight years old. I was working on the idea you hated kids or at least would refuse to be a stepmother. I thought wrong, and I'm sorry."

"I don't hate kids, Ash. I never did, but at seventeen, of course, I damn well didn't want the responsibility of someone else's kids again. Now I'm all grown up. Things are different."

"That may be, Rylee, but your hostility toward Arden and the insistence I dob her in about the doping puts me in a very awkward spot. Arden believes she can achieve selection in a couple of years and I can't scuttle that chance for her. Besides it would destroy my relationship with her, and Arden is the only mother Lilli has ever known. I can't take that away from her. I can't."

"Take her away from Arden and risk her with a stepmother. Me, perhaps? But then, I'm not someone who can be trusted with children, is that it? You couldn't trust me with Lilli?" Rylee asked, her tone sharp and censuring.

"Of course I would trust you. It's just I have an issue with stepmothers—mine in fact. Ruth always hated Arden, even though she loved me," Ash said.

"Really—someone who will teach your daughter right from wrong? Not like Arden, who cheats and brutalizes her horses to win. Is that what you want your daughter to grow up believing? Once upon a time, you would have been horrified."

They both fell silent as the waiter placed their food in front of them.

Immediately after the waiter had gone Ash leaned forward. "Oh for God's sake, lay off Arden and no, I don't want my daughter growing up believing anything goes as long as you win," he snapped.

She folded her arms under her breasts and glared at him. "Well, that's what is going to happen and the blame will ultimately lie with you."

"God damn it, you make such judgments on rumors. That's so bloody harsh."

The diners sitting at the table next to them frowned in their direction.

"Not just rumors. I saw the stuff she did to the horses before Aileen kicked her out. I caught her using spurs to hurt and a crop with a sharp end and rapping, amongst other things," Rylee announced in an undertone.

"Maybe so, but it's in the past," Ash protested in a low undertone. "She promised me she would never do anything like it again."

"Open your eyes, please," Rylee begged, as she pushed her untouched food away. "This is a mistake. I shouldn't have come tonight." She stood.

He watched her.

"I love you, Ash, but I cannot stand by and condone your sister's actions or your stubborn refusal to acknowledge what is really happening." She turned and walked away.

"Rylee."

She ignored him and hurried across the car park. As she went to open her car door, he gripped her shoulders tightly, turning her around to face him.

"I love you. Can't you just accept that's how it is?"

She shook her head. "No, I can't."

"For God's sake, Rylee. This is tearing me in two. I love you, I love Arden, and I love my daughter. For my sanity, can we reconcile the three, please?" He looked down at the ground then back up at her.

She stared unwaveringly into his eyes. She heard the sincerity in his voice and saw the desperation in his expression. Cynical amusement bubbled up in her chest. She tried to choke it back, but it forced its way out. She laughed so fervently her body trembled and tears pooled in her eyes. He stood still in front of her, staring at her.

It took a long while, but she finally forced herself to calm down and glanced at him. "Your sanity. Seems to be that matters to you? What *you* want. What *you* need. Other people have needs too, but they have to make do with what they can get—like this." She stretched up and covered his mouth with hers.

She caressed, sucked and nibbled at his willing flesh. He responded by grabbing her shoulders and slamming her against his chest. He slipped his hands under her shirt and pushed aside her lacy bra.

"I need you. I love you," he moaned against her skin.

With his swollen cock pressed against her abdomen, she wanted him so badly. She was tempted to open his fly and let him take her right there in the well-lit car park, but reason stayed her hand.

Without warning he scooped her up and strode away from her car.

"Where are we going?" she asked.

"Home," he said.

He wasn't even breathing heavily as they crossed the road, and into the lift. When the doors closed, he captured her mouth again before moving on to her cheeks, her neck and down her cleavage. He probably would have gone farther, but the lift clanged open. He strode along the verandah and, with fumbling fingers, he unlocked the door before shouldering his way into his apartment and heading into the bedroom. He put her down, but didn't let go of her.

He cradled her head with one hand and with the other undid her skirt and pushed it down. He kissed her deeply. She could taste him — wine and peppermint. He released her mouth for just a moment to lift her top and bra over her head. Clad in lacy panties, she undid his belt and pushed his pants down, exposing his upright cock. She sank to her knees in front of him and lightly licked the length of his hardened shaft. The tangy taste of male stimulated and heightened her senses as she circled her tongue around the head of his penis. Then she took his cock into her mouth all the way to the base of the shaft. She cupped his balls, reveling in the soft wrinkly flexibility of the skin covering them. They were firm to her touch and she rolled them between finger and thumb before she lowered her head and sucked each one through the pouch of skin. He moaned.

His fingers trailed through her hair before he cradled her head at his groin. She sucked and licked in a smooth up and down movement over the hot, satin smooth flesh of his cock. She tasted the salty tang of pre-cum. He pulled away from her and dropped to his knees beside her and gently eased her onto her back before he lay on his stomach between her legs. He pushed her legs farther apart and lowered his head between them. He ran his tongue over her flesh, dipping the tip in between the folds of her lips and the wet entrance to her pussy. The fiery tingle of arousal when he tucked his tongue up under the hooded flap and flicked it over her clit almost blew her mind. She moaned and whimpered under his thoroughly intimate ministrations.

Something firm and mobile slipped inside her — she guessed two or three fingers. He moved them in and out and turned them clockwise first then anticlockwise, making her muscles clench and spasm in response. She was barely conscious of the change from his fingers to his cock as he delved all the way in and lay there unmoving. Impatient, she gave a little lift with her hips to encourage his rhythm, clamped her legs around his waist and met his thrusts with tilts of her hips. A trail of tingling pinpricks scattered all around her vulva, right down to her butt. She clenched her legs and cheeks together and pulled the sensation deep inside, where it burst into an explosion of needle sharp points of pleasure. She bucked under its dominating rush, and Ash moved faster and deeper until all she could feel was the hard length of his cock plunging again and again into her tingling pussy. He groaned as he exploded inside her, and she gave into her own release, which rushed over her right to her head. Every hair she had stood on end and trembled under the onslaught until they collapsed on the floor together in a tangled sweaty heap — the only sound in the room, the rasp of their uneven breathing as they both fought for control.

"My love. You are so beautiful. So desirable," Ash murmured.

She cradled his face between her hands and pulled him down to her. She kissed him. A brief ardent kiss before she rolled away from him. He reached out to stop her. "Stay, Rylee. Stay the night with me," he begged.

"No."

Rylee was already partly dressed by the time he gave any indication he comprehended that she was going home to her own bed, he grasped her arm.

"Why are you going? There's no need," he protested.

"I have horses to feed and exercise in the morning. This is how it will be. We have separate lives to lead. I will not publicly acknowledge you while you support your sister's cruelties. And you have no intention of sharing your precious family life with me—not suitable step-mother material, I think you said. So a quick satisfying fuck now and again was your preferred arrangement, I believe."

He suddenly seemed older, tired and just a little bit unsettled. She wondered if he was re-assessing his decisions of the past and present and probing deeper into his psyche for the real truth he so far had refused to face. She wanted to hurt him at that moment, rub his excuses right into his soul.

"I said no such thing, and you know it. I said I was not expecting you to—"

"Goodnight." She ruthlessly cut off his excuses.

Despite her tough exterior and flippant dismissal of Ash as she departed, Rylee was swamped by despair, her stomach clenching and burning as she walked quickly back to her car. If this was how it was going to be between them, she had better toughen up or this charade of not caring would rend her in two.

Once she had crossed the road and unlocked the car, she glanced up at his apartment. He stood at the window watching her—a sad figure all alone, outlined by the mellow light behind him.

As she drove through the night, she wished fervently the feelings she had for Ash would go away. *It is all wrong. Why can't my heart understand what I know in my head?*

* * * *

Regan frowned as Rylee let herself in.

"I gather that didn't work out so well?" he commented.

Rylee pushed the door shut behind her and dropped her keys in the tray. "We argued about Arden and, of course, I couldn't help but tell him a few home truths about his precious sister. He didn't take it too well."

Regan held up the teapot and a cup, silently asking her if she wanted a cuppa. "Silly bugga. So will you see him again? Is he worth the heartache, Ry?"

She nodded yes to the tea and slumped into a chair. "I love him, but there seems to be too much between us. I don't know if it can be resolved and if the resulting hurt will be worth it in the end. And now there is the child, a daughter. I don't want the responsibility. I can't take on the responsibility. What if I fail again? Fail with his child?"

"God damn it, stop punishing yourself for what happened when you were twelve. You were just a kid."

"I know, but Rohan is still dead because of me and even if Ash does not know already, I will have to tell him."

"To be honest, Rylee, you don't. Today is not to be compared to then. Besides, if he turns away from you because of it then he's a bastard... Well, more than he already is."

Rylee sighed. "I am *so* confused."

"Sleep on it, sis. Maybe you'll see clearer in the morning if he is worth fighting for."

* * * *

Sleep on it. Well that was a nice thought. Rylee rolled over to the other side for the hundredth time since she'd climbed into bed. She tried to talk herself through the issue. All she had to do was close her eyes to what Arden was doing, pretend it had nothing to do with her – if it wasn't for the stables, of course. Could she turn her back on her godmother's dreams if it meant she could have Ash? A tiny voice inside whispered *yes, perhaps.* She analyzed it some more, but as soon as she came up against the horse abuse, she baulked. To stand beside Ash at an event and applaud Arden, knowing what she had done to achieve her goal… Rylee felt sick. There was no 'perhaps' in her mind. What she really couldn't understand was how Ash could be so blasé about it and let his daughter be exposed to such a dreadful example.

Sleep finally came drifting in just before dawn.

Chapter Five

Two of the horses Rylee had seen competing at the three-day event in the CCI2* were being offered for sale, due to the owner's university and work commitments, and they also had an endurance horse that appeared promising. Rylee was keen to add to her stables and believed the endurance horse, a half-brother to Arden's Cockatoo Ridge Jackaroo, would be excellent for one of her clients to go on with as she moved from junior endurance competitions to an open level.

When they arrived at the stables, Rylee could see a small huddle of people by the arena.

"I thought this was a private viewing?" she said.

"It was supposed to be. I'll go find out what Reg's up to."

Rylee followed her brother to the stables where Reg was saddling Boomerang Joe. He smiled as they walked up.

"Sorry, guys. The St. Clairs just turned up. Arden thinks she has first dibs on this fella because she already owns Cockatoo. I was a bit pushed to send them packing."

Regan shrugged and looked toward Rylee. "You want to give it a miss?"

She did, but she wasn't going to. Arden would not stop her pursuing her goals.

"No, but I want first ride. Poor horse won't be fit for anything after Arden's finished with him."

Reg nodded. "Fine by me. Why don't I just give you a leg up right here?"

Rylee nodded, pulled her helmet on, then using Reg's cupped hands for a leg up, swung up onto the big gray. She immediately liked the look of the solid shoulders and neck.

With a gentle squeeze, she asked him to walk forward. He was responsive to her aids and seemed light on the bit.

As she entered the arena, Arden jumped toward the gate. "Reg King, how dare you insult me like this. I came to see your damn horse — to ride it."

Reg shut the gate behind Boomerang. "Rylee had an appointment. She gets first refusal."

"Damn you," Arden shouted.

Rylee brought the big gelding around the arena in a collected trot then moved to a canter as she passed Ash and Arden by the gate. Arden's face was scrunched up in a livid mask, her eyes flashing sparks of fury. Ash met her gaze with a smile and a nod of what seemed like approval. Although Boomerang was not specifically a dressage horse, he'd had some training and moved through each of the requirements of the test smoothly when Rylee asked. With him warmed up, she turned him toward the jumps, and with a steady, considerate approach, he cleared each one. Rylee liked him. He was big, steady, educated and the vet had cleared him yesterday. She decided she would buy.

She brought the gray to a slow walk and halted at the gate. "I'll have him, Reg."

Arden screeched.

Ash grabbed her arm. "Enough, Arden. You don't really need him. I'll get you something superior."

Arden flung away from her brother and stalked toward their car.

Ash walked up to the fence. He stroked Boomerang's nose. "You look good on him. He's a nice animal and he should serve you well in the stables. Perhaps you should think about riding in endurance."

Rylee remained mounted. It felt safer that way. Every inch of her was melting with desire and her hands trembled on the reins. All she could think about was the feel of his cock thrusting into her body and the buzz of arousal that carried her to heaven and back. From where he stood, she could smell his distinct fragrance, and see his chest rising and falling as he breathed. His riding pants clung to his legs, crotch and backside, leaving nothing to the imagination. His hand rested on the bridle right in front of her face, so close she could see the tiny hairs on his bare arms glinting in the sunshine. She struggled to draw breath.

"We can work it out, Rylee. Please don't give up on me," he muttered.

"Ashford, are you coming?" Arden's strident voice snapped the spell between them.

"You better go."

"Rylee?"

She shook her head. "Just go to your sister. You've made your choice."

His shoulders slumped as he turned and walked toward the car. She watched him leave and inside she sobbed for what she had lost. As his car disappeared around the corner, she followed Reg back to the stables. Both she and Regan put the other horses through their paces, but Rylee was undecided. Both needed work in dressage and the smaller of the two seemed to have some hesitation when jumping. Not quite sure, she arranged to return the following week if the horses were still available.

* * * *

When they arrived, the sun had just peeped over the thick wall of pine trees that made up the edge of the forest. She parked the big four-horse float in a flat shady spot and quickly unloaded Zea, Monti and Boomerang.

Rylee loved the atmosphere at endurance competitions — the sound and smell of the horses, the fresh air and the coiled excitement and energy. Aileen had been encouraging two of her clients, Sophie and Tayla, for almost a year to give endurance riding a go and finally, six months ago, they had agreed. Rylee had picked up their training where Aileen had left off. She and the girls had worked diligently to be ready with both themselves and the horses at peak fitness.

During the last couple of weeks, Rylee had ridden Boomerang Joe, had really enjoyed their outings and had bonded well with the horse. She had toyed with the idea of joining her two clients competing as novices in this limited distance endurance ride through Kypo forest. Regan had encouraged her, so she'd put an entry in.

When the girls arrived in the cool darkness of dawn, she had unloaded her own gear and her horse. She felt alive and excited with anticipation. It had been so long since she had ridden competitively. While Rylee hadn't had long with Boomerang, Reg had assured her he was well conditioned. She had entered him in the intermediate and planned to take it steady.

She hoped they had done enough for the two young women to make a respectable showing. A decent result would certainly help Rylee's business and boost their confidence. All three horses had been vet checked, approved and the three women stood, quietly talking strategy for dealing with the course, the water crossing and the uphill stretches. Rylee emphasized to both girls waiting for the call to start, the need to preserve the horses well-being.

A bark of chilling laughter shattered the quiet moment between readiness and starting. Rylee didn't need to turn around to identify the owner. A burning rage burst into flames and swept through her like wildfire. *Damn Arden.* She turned around to find her towering over her, astride a tall, muscular horse. It snorted and threw its head around, a wild light in the deep depths of its brown eyes. Rylee stepped back. She read the tightness in the horse's stance and the resentment in its expression.

"So, Rylee, you decided you could compete with me, now you have a decent nag? I thought you would have had more sense."

In a deliberate attempt to frustrate her nemesis, she ignored the jibe and attempted to be more than civil. "Good morning, Arden. Is this one of your new horses?"

"It is. Shamal of the Desert. Ash bought him for me just for endurance. He's much better quality than Reg's old nag."

Rylee studied the animal. "He appears edgy," she said.

Arden waved one gloved hand in the air and smiled. "He's keen. That's all."

"Mmmmm. Very nice conformation. He should be well suited to the task," Rylee commented politely. *With a different rider perhaps and before he was ruined.*

"My brother always makes sure I have the best," Arden crowed from her perch.

"Of course. Now, if you don't mind, I have to prepare the girls for their start."

"So, you're riding?" Arden asked, looking around at the gathered equipment and the tethered horses.

"Yes, I am, but you will still have a clear run to the winner's trophy today because I'm entered in the intermediate section," Rylee snapped, unable to maintain the false civility a moment longer.

Arden's laughter barked out again. Bystanders ogled her, curiosity on their faces. "You would never be in my way to the winner's ring. You never were," Arden snarled.

"Damn it, don't be such a bitch," Ash growled as he walked up.

Rylee started at the harshness of his words as Ash come up behind the restive horse with a deep frown furrowing his brow.

"Well, it's true," Arden replied waspishly.

"Regardless, it's not necessary to make such comments," Ash snapped.

Arden pouted sulkily at her brother's rebuke.

Ash surveyed the fidgeting horse. "Go walk him around. He's jumpy."

With a sharp jerk on the reins, Arden turned her horse and trotted off. After a few more hints and suggestions, Rylee sent her girls on their way.

As she prepared to mount Boomerang, Ash came to stand beside her. "I won't stay because I know it's not good for your reputation, but I just wanted to wish you luck today. Boomerang should do you proud. You two look good together—like us," he said.

"Thanks for the support, but you know we'll never officially be together."

"Never say never. We can work it out," he replied.

She'd heard the bitterness in his voice and the sadness, but already people were staring. She expected there would be some extra scrutiny of her horses when they crossed the finish line because she had spoken to Ash and Arden. Probably Arden's whole reason for approaching her was to bring Rylee down, even if only by criminal association.

* * * *

Rylee buzzed with anticipation as she lined up to begin. It was a glorious morning—the air was crisp and fresh after the last couple of days' rain. She could feel Boomerang relaxed underneath her, but at the slightest command, he responded. He seemed keen, with eyes bright and his ears pricked forward.

Then she was off. The first leg of the course was a steady uphill rise along the old fire track between two huge stands of pines. There were plenty of obstacles left from the last lot of logging and the sprouting of new growth. Boomerang snuffled energetically and they cantered at a steady pace up the first rise. A steady increase in the steepness forced them to slow to a snappy walk. As they topped the rise, Rylee paused for a moment to admire the view and let Boomerang catch his breath. Then, with the slightest of indication from her, they set out at a trot across the summit of the hill then walked down the steep incline to the stream in the gully. The going was rough and Rylee took it steady, still not completely sure of her horse's ability. He didn't seem at all stressed by the exertion. The stream was fast moving and swollen from the rain, but the entrance into the water was flat and sandy. The other side was different and Boomerang hesitated before he leaped the first bank then scrambled the rest of the way. Rylee halted him at the top, not overly happy with his handling of the steep bank. She patted him and talked to him, and when he seemed more settled, they moved up the gentle slope at a steady canter. They seemed to be keeping up well with the rest of the horses, but she couldn't see Arden ahead of her and she knew she would not be behind. Most of the riders dismounted for the next particularly steep boulder strewn section and it was then that Rylee looked up and saw a still-mounted Arden pushing her horse hard as it struggled to top the escarpment. She was clearly in the lead. Rylee tried not to let it affect her mood, but she felt sorry for the horse and was embarrassed for Ash when she heard several uncomplimentary things said by other riders. Sophie and Tayla joined her where she waited for them at the top of the escarpment.

"You shouldn't have waited, Ry. You were doing so well," Tayla gasped, as they arrived.

She laughed. "Oh, I'm not fussed about winning today. It was more important that I check on how you two were managing. Are the horses both behaving?"

"Monti is, but Zea was a little spooked by a couple of roos. I nearly went flying when she shied, but she settled quickly."

"Okay. Well you better get moving. There are still a couple of tough stretches, so pace yourselves."

"Okay," they both chorused as they moved off together.

Boomerang's superior size and conditioning soon took him ahead. And again as they moved through stands of pine, Rylee saw Arden galloping ahead. Even from that distance, Rylee could see that Shamal was sweating. As she cantered up the rise, there was a movement to her right and four kangaroos bounded out of the trees in front of Boomerang. He snorted and baulked slightly, but moved on when Rylee signaled he should. Rylee was feeling her muscles and bones by the time she could make out the finishing line down the gully, but the big horse barely seemed to be sweating. She rode at a steady canter, only slowing to a walk as she reached the edge of the clearing. There was a splatter of applause as she dismounted and she caught a glimpse of Ash over the saddle, clapping enthusiastically. The vet checked her horse and approved him fit. She had come in fourth.

Almost an hour later, the first of the novices began coming in, and Rylee was thrilled to see one of her girls come in second and the other fifth. The horses were assessed fit and immediately bedded down in comfort while the three of them ate lunch. Tayla and Sophie rattled on and on about their rides and wanted to talk strategy until the horses from the open class began to trickle in one by one.

Arden arrived first, her horse sweating, jumpy and obviously distressed. Rylee noticed the vet made a thorough assessment of her horse. He sent the animal to a ten-minute yard and made Arden wait to the side. After ten minutes had elapsed, he called her back. Before he had finished, Ash strode over to where Arden was engaged in a heated discussion with the officials. He didn't appear at all pleased. Finally, the vet sighed and approved her horse's fitness. Arden was jubilant. Today was her day. She started to head in their direction, but Ash pulled her away with a few sharp words Rylee couldn't quite make out.

When Arden went to collect her trophy, the applause was a mere splutter and she scowled at those gathered around before she went to stand beside Ash. Ash just looked sad. Rylee applauded loudly when Sophie on Zea collected her second and Tayla, the fifth prize on Monti. She saw Ash applaud their success and hers. She returned his acknowledgment briefly.

It was soul destroying not to be able to go to him to share her success and her renewed desire to compete, with the man she loved. To have to snub him in public cut her to the core. She almost threw all she had worked for aside by going to him, but it wasn't just her who would be damaged by association, so she held herself tightly in check. She couldn't destroy the dreams of the two girls, because both had potential. It didn't matter how much she loved him. In the long run she could not give up her dreams either, just because he wouldn't face the truth. In the end she would be left with nothing. All the rationalization in the world didn't ease her pain. Her heart was heavy and her body sagged with misery induced fatigue and she struggled with the effort required to load the horses and equipment for the long drive home.

* * * *

The magpies warbled in the background, trying to encourage her to climb out of bed and drag herself through the shower. She should have been jumping for joy at the progress she had made with the stables, but instead she struggled to even get out of bed, weighed down by her decision to reject Ash. Her mind told her it was the right choice, but her heart disagreed. It had been almost a week since she had seen or heard from him and all she could do was get on with her rejuvenation of the stables and hope the hurt of separation eased with time.

* * * *

Today her new round of school classes started, and Rylee needed to keep her mind on the job. She completed her preparations in the stables for the class just as they arrived. She studied the girls in front of her—six of them, ranging from seven to nine years old. It was the first time students from the prestigious private girl's school, St Wilhelmina's, had taken the opportunity to participate in her school horse riding program. Rylee could barely contain her excitement. She now had five schools participating and three more interested. All the girls were keen and she matched them carefully with suitable ponies, based on the information sheets their parents and the children had filled out. They were all beginners, with Sarah, Chloe and Millie saying they had never even been near a horse before.

One girl stood out—she seemed somehow familiar. A tilt of the head, a smile or a phrase, Rylee couldn't place it. Annie appeared the most confident, so she paired her with one of her best ponies, an older, well-educated mare called Moonbeam. Once they had their horses, Regan went through feeding, grooming and safety before they were given a short ride around the undercover arena on lead ropes. Regan and Rylee worked diligently to make sure hands were placed correctly, stirrups adjusted, heels down and petting of horses encouraged. The girls were so excited when they got back on the bus, the teacher had trouble getting them to put their seatbelts on.

With the first session behind them, Rylee watched the bus leave, pleased with how it had gone, but she did wonder about Annie. She suspected the child of lying about her experience with horses, for despite her assurance she was a beginner, her grip on the reins had been a little too correct and that, along with her steady seat and legs at just the right angle, it all made Rylee suspicious. Besides that, she had had no trouble at all doing the pony's hooves where everyone else had struggled to even get the hoof off the ground, let alone wield the hoof pick effectively. She shrugged her suspicions away. It didn't really matter anyway.

She readied Dalton's Hope, mounted then went to work him in the arena, finding it peaceful in the covered arena with just her and the horse. The sounds of steady work, the horse breathing, the soft thud of hooves in sand, the squeak of leather and the occasional snort were relaxing.

Just as they finished working through the movements of the level two dressage test, Rylee gradually began to feel uneasy. She couldn't explain it, but she would have sworn she was being watched. As they finished the test, she turned the horse into the center and halted. She peered around and in the shadowed corner by the big doors, she saw her. A second too late, the intruder backed into the shadows.

Rylee couldn't see her face, but she knew it was Arden.

Rylee rode over to the railing closest to her. "What do you want?"

Arden stepped out of the shadows, and Rylee gasped at the savagery in the other woman's expression.

Arden strutted right up to the fence. "I've come to warn you to back off, O'Shaughnessy. Stay away from my brother. You're nothing but trouble."

"What is between your brother and me has nothing to do with you," Rylee replied. She sounded calm, but on the inside she quivered with unease. She knew this woman thought nothing of hurting people, especially those who stood in her way.

Arden gripped the top rail of the barrier with the clawing fingers of one hand. "Anything to do with Ash is my business, especially when it's you." As she brought her other hand up, Rylee realized Arden held a stock whip. Cold fear shivered down Rylee's spine. She had no idea how Dalton would take this situation.

"You will not bring me down," Arden announced. "I'm too smart for you."

"You think so. You think it is smart to dope your horses and use cruel aids in training? To push them to collapse like you did at the weekend? That poor bloody horse was almost done in. Even the vet wasn't happy."

Arden glared up at her. "It gets the results I want. That's smart. Not like you. I won."

"There is no honor in the way you won—no honor at all," Rylee sneered back at her enemy.

"Look at you. There is no honor in working with tame or broken down nags so you can teach people to ride that should never pull on a pair of jodhpurs.

Where did your ambition go?" Arden asked. "That heat in the blood we once shared, to make it to the top."

"It died the day I saw you abusing your horses. The day I realized that this is what you did to win. To hold that gold trophy in your hand and hang a ribbon on the poor, abused horse's neck. My passion for competing died with the death of your horse, Lord of the Manor," Rylee replied.

"For Christ's sake, it was only a horse and not a very good one, or it would have finished the course first," Arden snapped back.

"I'm not like you, and I never will be."

"No, you're not in the same class as me or my brother. Stay away from him, or I'll make you sorry you ever returned."

"Really?"

"You're not good enough for him or my niece. Lilli regards me as her mother. I love her. I will never let you take her away from me. Do you hear? Never," Arden said.

Rylee was stunned by Arden's wild accusation. "I don't want to take her away from you. Whatever gave you that idea?"

"Yes, you do, and you don't even like kids. You wouldn't love her like I do. You can't have her, do you hear? You can't have Lilli."

With sudden ferocity, Arden stepped sideways and advanced through the opening with the whip swinging in her hand. *My God, she means to attack me. The mad bitch has lost the plot.* She cracked it above Dalton's ears. He flinched, but stood his ground. Rylee sank deep in her seat. The lash cracked again. It clipped the horse's ears. The terrified horse screamed and backed up, throwing his head up and down.

Rylee turned him away and trotted to the other side of the arena. Arden advanced swiftly toward the agitated horse. The sharp cracks shattered the stillness of the enclosure and echoed around the unlined roof.

"Why are you doing this?"

A sharp cackle came from the woman in front of her. "To teach you a lesson, you little Irish madam. You can't have my brother or my niece. They're mine. Do you hear me? Mine."

She tried to drive them up against the wall, but Rylee turned the gelding to face the woman on the ground and signaled for him to go forward. Dalton responded, leaping in a canter to charge at Arden. She turned and slashed with the whip. It caught Rylee across the shoulder and slapped onto the horse's rump as they passed. The horse shied, half reared and squealed his protest. Despite the fact Rylee barely clung to her seat, she kicked the horse on. "Go, boy, go." He surged forward, eager to get away from the scary person dishing out the unexpected pain. Rylee heard Arden laughing from behind them. Her heart thumped. Sweat ran down between her breasts and her breath came in tiny little gasps.

She didn't rein the horse in until they'd arrived back at the stables. At the big stable door, she threw herself out of the saddle and turned to peer through gathering gloom, terribly afraid Arden would follow her. There was no sign of her, but moments later she heard the roar of a powerful engine and saw car lights flash as Arden's little yellow sports car negotiated the dip outside the gate.

She led Dalton into the stall and let him stand as she clutched the wall for support and rested her head against the cool timber. Her knees had turned to jelly and tremors shook her. Her mind raced in circles. She didn't know what to think and if it wasn't for the stinging pain in her shoulder, she would struggle to believe the attack had actually happened. Not for the first time, Rylee wondered about Arden's mental state. Despite evidence Arden had gone, she decided to close the doors and put the bar across. Her hands were shaking so much she struggled to undo the girth, especially when Dalton fidgeted. Finally, she pulled it off and placed it on the dividing wall then swapped the bridle for a head collar. All the time, with wary glances toward the door, she picked his hooves then began to brush him with the dandy brush. She was absolutely furious. How dare that woman come to her home and attack her — put her and the horse at risk. The only reason Arden would try and frighten her out of Ash's life was if she really was still involved in dodgy practices. She knew that if her brother chose Rylee, her career was finished and she was determined that wouldn't happen. *Well, attacking me was a wasted effort because her brother was the only one who could denounce her.* She debated calling the police but decided against it. This was personal, between her and Arden, and she cringed away from the thought of bringing more disrepute to Ash.

By the time she had finished brushing Dalton and putting his rug on, she had calmed a bit, but determination had hardened in her mind. She would somehow make Ash see his sister's faults.

She could barely move her shoulder under the searing burn of the welt left by the whip, but she managed to climb into the loft to retrieve another rug for Dalton. Suddenly overcome with shock and sadness, she sat hunched on the bales of hay for quite a while in the dimly lit stable loft, mulling over her predicament. No easy answers came to mind and she had to ask herself if this man was worth all the angst and misery. Why couldn't she just turn off the feelings she had for him? It was a hopeless situation with little chance for a good outcome and yet she pined for him. Her ears strained to hear his voice, her nose to breathe in his scent and her seeking fingers to feel the satin firmness of his skin under her teasing strokes. Her need for him flowed through her veins like an addictive toxin. A little would never be enough. Warm tears trickled down her cheeks at the unfairness of it all. Surely love should not be this complicated.

The stable door creaked then clicked shut. She guessed it was Regan.

"I'm up here in the loft. Be down in a moment." She hurriedly wiped the moisture off her cheeks and hauled the rug down off the rack. She turned toward the ladder and came face to face with the object of her misery.

She hugged the cotton rug close to her chest and glared at him over it. "You shouldn't be here. You should have called."

He grimaced. "I know, but I didn't want you forbidding me to come."

"Why have you come? To check on your sister's handiwork?" Rylee challenged him.

"Arden's handiwork?"

"She was here earlier. She whipped me—and my horse."

"Arden's in Melbourne this week," Ash responded.

Rylee shook her head. "No, she's not."

When he ignored her protest, a deep seated uneasiness slithered over her. It had begun when Arden had first appeared in the arena and now growled menacingly in the back of Rylee's mind. Just what lengths would this woman go to keep them apart?

Rylee saw the disbelief in Ash's expression, but she was determined to make him see the truth.

"She *was* here." She swiveled on the bale and pulled her shirt off her shoulder. The red welt from the whip and the tiny beads of blood showed clearly, even in the dim light of the loft. "See this? This is her handiwork."

He stepped up close behind her to examine her injury, and her body buzzed with awareness, soaking up the warmth that radiated from him.

His fingertips were cool and gentle as he stroked her shoulder. "I don't understand. I don't believe you would lie to me, but I put Arden on the plane for Melbourne last night. She is not due back until the end of the week.

"She was here not more than an hour ago."

He gripped her shoulders. His desperate sexual need seeped from his body into hers. She could sense his confusion and uncertainty. Most of all she could sense his need for her.

"Say what you mean. Arden is still between us, and you're never going to let it die, are you? You will do anything to blacken her in my eyes."

"Damn you. I don't have to do anything except make you see. Open your eyes and see, for God's sake."

"It's not that simple, and you know it," he growled from behind her.

The heat from his body radiated across her back. As he pressed against her, she felt his erection and the touch of his hands as he stroked her shoulders and up the nape of her neck—warm and enticing. But the issue of Arden created a barrier between them. She felt it, even if he didn't, and she knew his desire to fuck her was not going to demolish it today.

She shrugged. "I know. It was simpler ten years ago and we couldn't fix it, then why do you think we can fix it now?" she asked. Her voice sounded dead even to her, a sign she was resigned to defeat, and a faint echo of how she felt inside.

"I'm not prepared to let what we have between us die. Please help me."

"There's nothing I can do. Only you can fix the mistakes of the past and revive it," she warned.

"You don't intend to make this easy for me, do you," he accused.

"Why should I?" she asked.

"Fair enough, considering this mess is mostly my own making. It pleased Arden greatly when you disappeared. She introduced me to her friends. Julie was one of them. She got pregnant, so we married. It seemed the right thing to do. Julie got caught up in Arden's world and the baby got left with the nanny or me. It wasn't until after Julie died that Arden became attached to Lillian. They are like mother and daughter. I can't destroy that. I can't."

"Even if it means you stay branded a horse doper. Even if it means there is no future for us? Why have you come to 'talk'? We both know there is nothing to talk about. You've made your decision. Arden will always come first."

"But I'm in love with you. I want you in my life. I don't care how."

"Well I do care. I might sound like an old romantic, but I want it all — the love, the romance, wedding and children. You know how, but you won't do that." She sighed. "Until you do, we can't be together in a relationship. I'm also not interested in some furtive affair that is both demeaning and repugnant, waiting for someone to denounce *me* as a horse doper. I can't close my eyes to what Arden does. I might as well condone it." Rylee took a deep breath at the end of her tirade. She wanted to cry, but she was too burnt out to give in to tears.

"Forget Arden. Forget the equestrian world. Forget my daughter. Just for a short moment, let it be just us." He stood and pulled her up with him. He moved forward until they were touching.

She squirmed out of his hold and stepped back. "This is not helping, Ash. It changes nothing."

"But it stops you thinking about all the ifs and buts," he said.

She laughed. "Just for a split second—a brief moment in time. That is no good to anyone, least of all me."

"Rylee?"

She stayed silent. She could hear him shuffling his feet in the loose hay on the floor.

He pulled her back to him and kissed her lingeringly. She gave into the pressure he applied and welcomed him to taste her as his lips crushed hers. He cradled her face and held her motionless so he could plunder her mouth. He slid his hand up through her hair and entangled them in her curls. "You're so beautiful, my sweet Rylee."

It would be so easy to give in, to sink so deeply into his desire that nothing else mattered, but she need to put a stop to this. If they had sex, nothing would be resolved. They couldn't move forward and the cycle would be never ending. She almost cried out in anguish knowing she had to send him away. "You need to go, Ash." She pushed him from her.

He clung to her. "I don't want to go. I want to love you. Don't send me away, just because of Arden."

"This is not about Arden. It's about you. You stand there and practically call me a liar and in the same breath, you profess to love me, plead to fuck me."

"You have doubts about my love?"

She nodded. "I'm sorry every time you take your sister's side and refuse to accept her innate badness — even tonight with the evidence right here." Rylee flashed her injured shoulder at him. "You don't believe that Arden was here. I can't live with that, Ash. The man I choose to share my life with has to give me not only his love, but also his loyalty, his trust and his integrity. Without it there is no value in the love given. You wouldn't give me that ten years ago and you won't give it to me now."

"It was one mistake," he groaned. "I have always been there for her, protecting her from our stepmother, protecting her from herself. She's not strong like you."

"Oh bullshit. She's taking you for a ride and you're letting her by believing her lies."

"But I put Arden on the plane myself. I don't understand how she could possibly be here and yet…" His words faded and his frown deepened.

"Well, who do you think whipped me? Do you think I did it to myself?" Rylee yelled.

"I am not saying I don't believe you, but… Oh shit, this is such a mess…" he cried.

"Just go, before you dig yourself into an even deeper hole," Rylee urged.

"Can I see you again?" he asked.

"I don't think that would be wise, considering. Go home to Arden and Lillian. Forget me. It's never going to work," she replied.

He shook his head, but backed off. "I can't accept this, Rylee. I *will* find a way to make it work." His face was gray and haggard. Confusion and pain shadowed his eyes as he paused for a moment and stared at her over the edge of the loft. "Rylee, just let me love you, kiss you. Then it won't matter. Please?" When she failed to back down from her demand, he disappeared from sight without another word.

Rylee stayed in the loft for quite a while after Ash had left. Finally, no closer to reconciling her hurt or her burning desire, she climbed down and went to work on Shannon, stroking his bay coat into satin shininess—brush stroke after brush stroke until sweat broke out on her skin and her arms ached with the repetitive action. Tears welled up and trickled down her cheeks as she threw her arm over the gelding's neck and she buried her face in his muscular shoulder. "What do I do, big boy? What do I do?" she muttered. "I can't seem to stop loving him."

Shannon nudged her with his nose and blew air against her leg. She stood for a long time in the darkness of the stable clinging to the solid warmth of the horse.

When she finally wandered up to the house, she found Regan lounging by the fire with two large pizzas on the table in front of him.

"Ah, about time you got in. The pizza's going cold, so tuck in."

Rylee turned and dropped her shirt off her shoulder. "Arden paid me a visit tonight with a stock whip in hand."

Regan leaped from the chair. "She what?"

Rylee nodded. "I was lucky Dalton's such a laid-back nag or it might have been worse."

"Damn that woman. Now what?"

"Nothing. Ash came. He didn't believe me. He damn well didn't believe it was Arden, because he put her on the plane to Melbourne. It's so humiliating. Despite the blatant evidence right under his nose, he practically called me a liar."

"You have to get over him, Rylee. Don't tell me you allowed him to…"

"No. I sent him away." Heat roared into her face. It was humiliating to have her baby brother asking if she'd had sex or not.

"Well, at least that's a start," Regan stated, flopping back in his seat and grabbing up a slice of pizza.

Chapter Six

The school classes continued and each time Rylee saw Annie ride, she was convinced the child had ridden before. On the second to last session, Rylee had set up some gymkhana games for the six girls to try. It was meant to be fun but before long, several of the girls had turned it into a competition. Everything went well until Annie lost the second race. At the end of the session, Annie was sulky and grumpy and being rough with the pony while she unsaddled and groomed her.

"Annie, do you have a problem with Moonbeam?" Rylee asked, struggling to keep her temper.

"Yes, she's too slow. She should have moved faster during the barrel races. I urged her to." Annie pouted up at Rylee.

"Well, Annie, Moonbeam is a good horse, and she did her best. You shouldn't take your disappointment out on her just because you didn't win."

Annie snorted and threw the hoof pick back in the grooming box. "Maybe I should have a faster horse — a better horse."

Something about the words jabbed on a nerve deep inside. Rylee flinched, but bit down on the angry retort that almost spilled out. She didn't want to lose the whole school because she snapped at one child.

"Maybe you should learn to ride better first, Annie. I saw today you weren't always giving Moonbeam the correct aids because you were so focused on winning. You actually confused her. You have to take part of the responsibility for losing."

Annie contemplated Rylee for a moment. "I need a better horse. That's all. Can I have a better one next session? I'm sure I would do better if I just had a better quality horse."

Rylee looked down at the child with a stern expression. "No, Annie. You will finish this term off with Moonbeam. You need to improve your riding before I upgrade you to the next level. I need to be sure you can handle a more difficult horse or you might just have an accident."

"Whatever," Annie muttered then shrugged and walked off.

* * * *

A week later when the class returned, Annie remained surly and very insistent that she needed a better horse.

"Annie, you either ride Moonbeam or you can sit here with your teacher for the whole session," she said calmly.

"Fine," Annie snapped then stomped off to the stable to prepare her horse.

From the moment the class entered the arena, Rylee could see from the jig-jogging and the ears flattened back against her head that Moonbeam was not herself.

Annie appeared to be doing the correct things, but just every now and again, Rylee saw her tug roughly on the bit and tap her heels sharper than she needed to.

With slow precision, the whole class moved through the formal exercises, but Moonbeam became more jumpy and Rylee could see Annie seemed to be having trouble controlling her. And the small pony was lathering up, which she never did. When they moved to the competitive exercises, Moonbeam rushed around the barrels and galloped over the finish line ahead of all the others but totally out of control, pulling on the bit and shaking her head. In the wake of Annie's mad dash to the winner's line, three barrels lay on their sides in the sand. Annie struggled to hold Moonbeam in a walk when they returned to the starting line for a second go. Rylee became more uneasy. Moonbeam never played up and she never went so fast as to knock the barrels down. Fearing an accident, she called a halt to the class and walked up to Annie. She soothed the agitated pony.

"Dismount, Annie," she instructed.

"Why?" the child asked, in an insolent tone.

"Because Moonbeam is upset. She never gets upset, so I need to know what is worrying her now."

"Stupid horse," Annie muttered, as she swung down from the saddle.

She stood back as Rylee moved in to examine the horse. Shock held her still and silent for a moment as she gaped at the bloodied hand she had stroked the horse's side with. She held out her hand to Annie. "What's this?" Rylee snapped in an icy cold tone.

"Blood," Annie replied nonchalantly.

Rylee glared down at the child. Annie glared back.

"I know it's blood," Rylee said. "How did Moonbeam come to be bleeding?"

"Well, if she didn't go so slow, I wouldn't have had to use them so much. She should have gone faster," Annie shouted.

"What have you used, Annie?"

Annie looked her right in the eyes. Rylee saw no shame or embarrassment in the little girl's eyes, just triumph.

"I used these," she announced and lifted one foot to show Rylee her boots. "It made her go faster and we won."

"You won, did you?" Rylee asked. "With three barrels down, I figure you lose. Barrels is a game of skill first, then speed. You got to cross the finish line by torturing a sweet-natured little pony. How dare you say you won," Rylee shouted.

She grabbed Annie's arm with no warning and, taking the horse's bridle in the other hand, she dragged her from the arena.

"Take over, Regan," she instructed her brother, who was standing silently by the rails.

The teacher stood as they approached, a deep frown furrowing her forehead. "What is this, Miss O'Shaughnessy? You have no right to manhandle the children like this."

"Really, Ms. Winters? Annie should think herself lucky she only has my fingers on her arm. Look at the horse. Examine her sides. She's bleeding. She's in pain. This child has illegally brought spurs to the session and used them on *my* horse. I do not tolerate animal cruelty."

"Oh dear. Annie. What have you done?" Ms. Winters flushed a deep red.

"I wanted to go faster," Annie whined.

"Get this child's parent here immediately," Rylee ordered.

"Don't call my dad. Call my aunty, please," Annie begged.

"This is not a job for an aunty, Annie." Ms. Winters dialed the number she had on the list.

Annie grabbed her teacher's arm. "Please don't call my dad," she pleaded.

"What is going on?" Ms. Winters put the phone to her ear.

The child burst into tears. "I'm not supposed to come riding. Dad will be furious," she cried.

"Mr. St. Clair—Ms. Winters. You are needed at Greenwood Stables immediately. It is a matter of upmost urgency regarding your daughter, Annie. Sorry...Lillian."

An icy chill ran down Rylee's spine. For God's sake, Annie was Ash's daughter. The spurs had to be Arden's. A wave of nausea rushed over her. Her stomach clenched and her chest cramped at the thought of the wrath that was to come. The expected confrontation with Ash would bring all the lies out into the open and he would be forced to acknowledge his sister's practices. Would that inevitability drive a wedge between them that they would never recover from? Probably, but it didn't really matter, for their love was doomed anyway.

The other girls had finished their lesson and were gathering by the bus when half an hour later Ash hurried into the stable yard. He looked from Rylee to Annie then to the teacher.

His face was red and his eyes manic as he stared from one to the other. "What the bloody hell is going on here. Lilli, what are you doing here? Ms. Winters, explain?"

"Dad, I just wanted to ride. You wouldn't let me," Annie wailed.

"You have an explanation? Why is my daughter here without my express permission?"

"Your sister signed her permission slip. Here. See for yourself. She signed it like she has on many other occasions." Ms. Winters held out the form with a trembling hand.

Ash snatched it from her and studied it with a glare distorting his face. Then he turned to Rylee. His expression didn't soften one bit.

"And do you plan to tell me you didn't realize this was my child?"

"Yes, Ash, I am, seeing you didn't have the manners to introduce us properly and she calls herself Annie."

"I hate my name Lillian. Everyone at school calls me Annie," the child cried.

Ash sagged. The heat of his rage seemed to slip away from him. "So, why have I been called? Obviously she's not hurt," he snapped.

"No, she's not hurt, but my horse is," Rylee stated bluntly.

Ash glanced from Rylee to Annie to the pony. "What?"

"Annie — or should I say Lillian — is wearing a pair of boots with nasty pointed spurs. She rode with them and has ripped Moonbeam's sides open. She's lucky not to have been thrown off. The poor horse is distressed and I have a vet coming to treat her."

Ash looked at Annie's boots, frowned then he bent down and picked up one foot. He let his child's foot drop to the ground as if he had been bitten. "But where would she have...?"

"For God's sake, open your bloody eyes. Where do you think she got them from? Your sister. Your pure and innocent sister. The one who never treats her horses badly. It's time you faced the truth," Rylee declared.

His face paled to a sickly gray, but he only glared at Rylee before he turned to Lillian. "Explain, right now, young lady. Where did you get them and why did you use them?"

"Daddy, I'm sorry. The horse was too slow. It's what Arden uses when her horses are too slow. They were in her wardrobe, so I took them. I wanted to go faster. I wanted to win."

"You wanted to win!" Ash grabbed Annie's arm in a fierce grip and dragged her toward the pony. "You wanted to win and to do that you did this to an innocent animal? You did this, Lilli? Oh my God, I have never been so ashamed."

"Well, Arden does it and you never get cross at her. You always buy her faster and better horses. So why are you mad at me?" The child's words choked into silence as she stood there peering up at her father, an expression of confusion twisting her face.

He took his hand off his daughter's arm. He stood by her in stunned silence, his head hanging almost against his chest. His eyes closed. "Go back to school, Lilli. We'll talk about this later."

The child turned away from her father, but instead of going toward the bus, she ran toward the injured pony and swung into the saddle with one lithe movement—that could only have been taught by Arden—onto the injured horse and kicked its sides. Moonbeam squealed then spun around and took off at a gallop toward the open paddocks.

"Regan, give me your horse," Rylee shouted.

She swung into the saddle and urged the horse forward. With a bounding leap, Thor galloped after the little silver mare. Rylee's heart pounded. If

Moonbeam took it into her head to buck or jump any of the fences, Annie would come off and, with the sharp spurs jagging at her tender sides, it was more than likely the little pony would. To make matters worse, Annie had thrown her helmet to the ground while she'd waited for her father.

Rylee heard thudding hooves behind her and glanced over her shoulder. Ash, mounted on one of the bigger ponies, was trying to catch up. She waved her hand and veered to the right. If she could get across the stream and in front of them, she could stop them before they reached the bridge. She could see, even from this distance, that Annie had no control over the little horse. Moonbeam galloped madly, her head shaking and flicking froth from side to side in a desperate attempt to escape the pain. Rylee lost sight of them for a moment as she charged through the gums by the stream where she kept her head down over the horse's neck to avoid low hanging branches. Fortunately, her horse slowed when it was faced with the steep bank down into the stream and she leaned back a little and let the horse pick its own path. Once across the shallow water course, the big gelding surged ahead and Rylee bent over his neck, encouraging it to bound up the other side of the stream bed. She urged Thor on, craning her neck to catch a view of the runaways, but she couldn't see Annie. At full gallop she crossed back across the bridge toward the bolting pony just before Annie and a sweat-lathered Moonbeam thundered up the ridge. She raced her horse in from the left front and Moonbeam started slowing immediately when she saw the bigger horse cutting across her path, so Rylee could grab the reins and pull to gently turn her.

They were almost at the bridge before Moonbeam halted. Rylee studied Annie's white tear-streaked face. She didn't quite know what to say. A scolding at this stage would not help the situation. Besides, it was her father's job to reprimand her.

"Thank God you're safe, Annie."

Gasping with exertion, Rylee jumped from the saddle. She let Thor go and walked quietly around Moonbeam. The little horse stood shaking and sweating, her breath gushing in and out of her tortured lungs in great grunts. Rylee reached up and helped the child down. Annie threw herself against Rylee where she stood hugging her and trembling as huge sobs convulsed her tiny chest.

"I'm sorry. I'm sorry," Annie cried.

Rylee put her arms around her shoulders and held her close. "So you should be, Annie. It is wrong to hurt a horse, but then you didn't really know, did you? Someone has taught you the wrong thing. It's not your fault."

Annie peered up at Rylee, tears still rolling down her cheeks. "Will you and Moonbeam forgive me? I won't ever do it again."

Rylee was so angry about the treatment her horse had been subjected to that a sliver of dislike for Annie remained, but she knew logically that this child had been misguided by someone she loved and trusted. She should not be punished for her actions. Rylee sighed, forgiveness was always a difficult thing, but valuable. "Yes, I will forgive you, Annie, but you will have to make a real effort to make amends to Moonbeam, because she won't trust you anymore."

"I'm sorry. So sorry," Annie sobbed, burying her face in Rylee's shirt.

Rylee eased Annie away from her, wiped the tears away and put her arms around her again. They watched together as Ash rode up. He leaped from the horse and pulled Lilli from Rylee's embrace. He knelt down so he could look directly into her face. He shook her none too gently.

"What the hell do you think you were doing? You could have been thrown off. I couldn't bear it if I lost you." Ash was so angry and distraught he spluttered his words, his face red, the veins prominent in his neck and his eyes filled with moisture.

Annie stood frozen in his clutching grip. She appeared almost afraid of him. "I'm sorry—sorry I used the spurs and sorry I ran away," she wailed. "I didn't mean to scare you."

Ash held his daughter at arm's length and glared at her. "What in the hell made you use those stupid spurs in the first place?"

Rylee desperately wanted to step in between father and daughter. She wanted to shout at Ash that it was his fault. Were his eyes open yet? But she didn't move, just stood frozen to the spot watching the man she loved chastise his child.

Lilli glowered up at her father, her face pale and still. "Arden uses them. I didn't realize it was wrong because you never tell Arden off. She uses them all the time and whips and stuff. She says it improves their performance." The defiant expression on the child's face disintegrated and Lilli blubbered in earnest now.

"I'm sorry, sweetheart, I had no idea Arden used them. She shouldn't." He loosened his grip on his daughter's arms and dropped his hands to his thighs.

Lilli wiped the tears away with her sleeve. "But she does and you watch her train, but you don't say anything."

Ash looked shamefaced, turned and walked away from his sobbing daughter, shaking his head. Rylee stepped forward and wrapped her arms around the child, wishing Ash could have brought himself to comfort Lilli, despite her wrong doing.

"Annie... Sorry, Lilli. It's not right to use things that will hurt a horse, especially when you are new to riding and not trained to use special equipment like spurs. Besides, I don't allow people to use that sort of equipment on my horses. I don't believe a good rider needs them," Rylee said quietly, watching for some reaction from Ash.

"I'm sorry. I never meant to hurt Moonbeam," Annie said again, fresh tears filling her eyes.

"I know. Now we need to take Moonbeam back to see the vet."

Lilli peered over Rylee's arm at her dad where he stood staring out over the horizon, his shoulders set square and stiff. "What about my dad? Will he still be angry with me?"

Rylee patted Lilli's shoulder. "I think maybe your dad and you will need to have a chat about what has happened. Now up you go on my horse. You can ride behind me."

With Moonbeam on the lead and Lilli up behind, Rylee guided the big gelding toward the stables.

Ash mounted his horse without saying anything to either of them. He rode a little ahead. Even though she was angry at him, Rylee couldn't help but be concerned for him and the shame he must carry. He obviously had plenty to think about—how his blind eye to his sister's excesses had now affected his daughter. To be sprung by one's child in what amounted to a lie must have been one of the most shattering experiences in the world. Children could be less than forgiving of parent's transgressions and failures. Ash would have some bridges to mend.

Ash's heart still beat madly while his lungs struggled to get enough breath. He was furious at himself, Annie and Arden and that was a reasonable response, but he couldn't justify why he was also angry at Rylee for not recognizing his daughter, for letting her ride and for being so damn reasonable about the whole bloody disaster—her injured horse, his daughter's unforgivable transgression and him for being so damn blind.

His heart had almost exploded with terror at the sight of his daughter being carried off at a mad gallop. In his mind, he could see Julie clinging desperately to the neck of the bolting horse in the same manner. Her frantic screams for help unanswered as he and Arden had failed to catch up to her and the bolting horse before it had charged a six rail fence, baulked, crashed into the railings then thrown Julie over its head. She had never regained consciousness.

Shame had seared his soul in the face of Lilli's accusation that he let Arden do it. He castigated himself for being so blind, so loyal to his baby sister. He had spent so many of his formative years protecting her from their stepmother's dislike. How did one just stop doing that?

His eight-year-old daughter's allegations were a childish echo of Rylee's. He didn't know what to say to her. How could he defend himself to his child and punish her for what he had condoned. *Oh God, what a bloody mess I've made of everything.*

No wonder Rylee was so angry with him. He hadn't listened to her before or more recently. He had brushed her concerns aside. Again and again he had put Arden first and now he was reaping the rewards — betrayal, lies and lost love.

He didn't know what to say to Rylee — the woman he loved. The woman whose integrity and trust he had questioned and betrayed. He thought of the day ten years ago when he had gone to the stables to find Arden, and had then been discovered by Rylee and Aileen Jones holding a bottle full of performance enhancing drug and an empty syringe. The immediate assumption had been made that he was the one doing the injecting, and even though he had just at that moment snatched the stuff off his sister, he had let them believe it was him to save Arden's equestrian dream. He knew he'd looked guilty that day and even felt it, but that was nothing on his guilt now, riding a few meters in front of his traumatized and confused daughter. Then he had been innocent — today he was not. His face burned with the shame.

His shame turned to rage as he rode — rage against the sister he loved. Who he had taken the rap for. The sister, who had lied to him then, and was lying to him still.

The horse danced underneath him, soaking up the fury that trembled through his body. He tried to calm himself, but found it impossible. Last night he had defended Arden and practically called Rylee a liar. How could she ever forgive him such a huge transgression? He would have enough trouble forgiving himself for being a fool.

He reined in at the saddling yard, tied his tired horse up and walked to the gate. He stood there staring down the driveway wishing fervently for escape. Moments later, Rylee and Annie halted. Regan helped Annie down then took the horse from Rylee. Ash did not turn around. He felt exposed, standing alone in the stable yard unable to face the two people behind him. He didn't know what to say — and he would not try to justify himself. Ms. Winters peered under her brows at him and he turned away from her questioning stare.

He didn't know what to say to her either. He was mad at Lilli for lying, mad at Arden for deceiving him — for going against his express instructions — and mad at himself for being so slack that he didn't check just what his child had been given permission for. So much for trust.

He heard a car screech through the gate and roar toward him. He saw Arden behind the wheel. *What the hell is she doing here? She's meant to be in Melbourne? Holy shit, she's here and I called Rylee a liar. What the hell is happening? God damn it. My life is out of control.*

Right behind her came the vet. Rylee stood by Lilli, her arm draped supportively over the child's shoulder. Ash flinched from the expression in his daughter's eyes, but the look in Rylee's was even more emotionally crushing. Here he saw compassion, love and concern, none of which he deserved. But shadowed in the depths he also saw a savage expression of hurt and resentment. This he did deserve, and it crushed him beyond belief that he had betrayed his love so badly.

"What the hell have you done to Lilli?" Arden stalked toward them, her piercing blue eyes fixed on Rylee. "Risked her life on some untrained nag. How dare you?" Arden didn't appear to notice Ash standing so stiffly to the side.

Knowing she was about to attack Rylee, he strode between them. "Shut up, Arden."

His sister turned. Her face paled. "What are you doing here?"

"I could ask you the same question, sister dear. Aren't you supposed to be in Melbourne? You've outright lied to me."

Arden waved her hand to dismiss the accusation. "Oh, I came back." She turned toward Rylee. "Lilli, come here to Aunty Arden. I will make it all better. Don't you worry."

Lilli glared at her aunt. "This is your fault—yours and Daddy's. You both lied to me."

"Whatever are you on about, sweetie?" Arden almost danced toward them in her stilettoes.

Lilli bent down, tugged off one of the offending boots and threw it toward Arden. It landed with a thud at her feet. "This is what I'm on about, Aunty Arden." The sarcasm turned the affectionate moniker into an insult not misunderstood by any of those gathered around. Ash stood immobile. Rylee squeezed Lilli tightly.

Arden bent down and picked up the boot. She examined it closely then fixed her niece with a penetrating stare. "Wherever did you get these nasty things?" she asked.

"They're yours," Lilli accused her aunt.

Arden flicked her head to one side, her expression drawn sharply into one of feigned disbelief. "These have nothing to do with me. What makes you say such a thing?"

"Because I got them out of your cupboard. They're yours. I've seen you use them before—on Black Satin," Lilli yelled and stamped her foot.

Rylee stepped forward. "For goodness sake, have the guts to own up to it. Stop blaming your eight-year-old niece for *your* crime, just like you blamed Ash ten years ago. You let your brother take the blame for your crime. You destroyed his riding ambitions to save yours."

"You petty minded, bitch, Rylee O'Shaughnessy. You think you've now got what you wanted all those years ago. Think again. Ash will never take your word over mine. Never," Arden screeched.

"Oh yes, he will," Ash said. "From now on, you wear your own dirt, little sister. Your lies don't wash with me anymore. Your lies put Lilli at risk. Your ruthless ambition at any cost has kept me from being with Rylee all these years. No more, Arden." The crushing pain in his chest as he cut his sister down was almost physical.

"Ash, you can't do this to me." She moved toward him, but he backed away and came to stand beside Rylee.

"I have, Arden. No more of your bullshit," he said.

"She doesn't want your kid, big brother. Don't forget that," she scoffed. "Will you throw Lilli to the wolves for her, like you're doing to me?"

"We'll work it out," Ash stated firmly.

"With Lilli as the sacrificial lamb? What sort of life will she have with a stepmother who doesn't want her? Who does not even like kids. Doesn't even want her own."

Rylee shivered. Arden was getting too close to her terrible truth. How could she be a stepmother? How could she take responsibility for another woman's child? Her carelessness had killed her little brother. She had been responsible for his care and safety and she had failed. It scared the heck out of her—the thought of being responsible for Ash's child. She felt sick at the idea.

Ash stared at Rylee with a desperate plea in his expression for her to dispute his sister's accusations.

She didn't need his urging. "Damn you, Arden. Just because at seventeen I said I didn't want children, you draw cruel assumptions."

Anger shuddered through her body. She did want children, her own children. But Lilli was a different matter altogether. All she knew was it could be her one chance to finally break Arden's hold on Ash and she had to take it, no matter what the consequences were.

"Well, you said it. You said you would never ever take on the task of being a stepmother."

Rylee gasped. Arden had hit the nail on the head without even realizing. She took a deep breath. Could she outright lie? Would it come back to haunt her if she did? How could she explain to Ash that she would not take responsibility for his daughter? Before she could compose an answer, Ash spoke.

"Arden, butt out."

"Shut up, big brother. You need to face the truth. She doesn't want to be a mother to Lilli."

"Rylee?" he asked.

"Ash, I... I... it's not that I don't want to be a stepmother. It's just I don't believe I would be good enough. I couldn't bear it if I disappointed the man I loved," she muttered the not quite lie between clenched teeth. She waited for God's wrath to come down upon her.

Nothing happened, except that Ash frowned. "Why would you disappoint, Rylee?"

She shivered. "I made so many mistakes with my siblings. It was such a wretched situation. Then I see my stepmother come in and take us all in hand. We gave her hell—so much and through it all she smiled, loved and cared for us. We eventually came to adore her. I don't think I'm woman enough to be half the stepmother she is and if I can't be as good, I would feel like I had failed—myself, the child and the man I loved. I couldn't bear it." Rylee cringed inside at the little twist to the truth.

Ash immediately wrapped his arms around her and pulled her into a tight embrace. "You are so tough on yourself, my love. You will make a great mother to any child, be it your own or another's."

If only you knew the truth, you wouldn't be saying that.

"Yes, sis. We never even noticed your stuff ups. We knew we were loved and our stomachs were always full of good food. What more does a kid need," Regan said from behind her.

"See," Ash said.

"Yes, but..."

"Shh, sis. Stop comparing yourself to Ma. She's one of God's angels," Regan announced.

Arden glared at them, her eyes sparking fury before she spun on her heel and stalked away. Moments later, her car roared out of the gate.

Ash sighed with relief. With Arden gone, he had a chance to perhaps make some amends. He would deal with her later without Lilli to witness the dressing down he intended to deliver. Things between them were going to be challenging enough as it was.

Chapter Seven

He glanced over to where Lilli stood by, watching the vet. "I think I might have some bridges to repair with my daughter. It is no more than I deserve. It will be good for me to eat some humble pie."

"Too right. In my opinion, Rylee is letting you off far too easily," Regan announced.

Ash looked up at Regan. "I know, but I'm sure you'll make up for her lack of censure."

"I might at that."

"Mr. St. Clair, I do need to get the children back to school. What is happening with, Lilli?" Ms. Winters asked.

"She can go back to school with you. I need to think about what has happened before I tackle Lilli."

"I understand," Ms. Winters said politely. "Lilli."

The child frowned at the teacher, but obeyed. She glared savagely at her father as she walked past him. Her disapproval cut him like a knife in his guts. How did a father *ever* earn a child's respect back when he had failed so absolutely?

"I'll see you soon, sweetheart. We'll have a chat then," he said.

"Whatever, Dad."

He wanted to chastise her for being insolent, but he let it go, not willing to add to her current dislike of him. It was more than he could cope with right now. When the bus disappeared out of the gate, he turned to Rylee. She appeared beaten. Emotions swirled in her eyes. She smiled, just a small sympathetic smile. He had some broken bridges to mend here too. God what had he done? How had he let his life get this out of control?

He stepped toward her. "I'm so sorry—for Lilli and the horse, for Arden and for being an idiot. Can you ever forgive me?"

"Right now, I don't know. I would like to think so, but I just don't know. I suppose it depends on what you do next."

"I'm so confused. I love Arden. She's my sister. But her betrayal really hurts. She used me and I willingly took the fall because I couldn't believe she could stoop so low. That she would be so under the spell of ambition. I'll have to sort her out."

"Well, your betrayal hurts me too—the fact you didn't believe me. You dismissed the evidence, preferring to believe your sister over me, the woman you profess to love so much. I don't know if I can ever trust you."

Ash glanced at the ground and ran his hand through his hair. When he looked back up at her he felt the life drain out of him under the burden of trepidation that he had lost his place in Rylee's heart forever. "Please don't say that. I know I'll have to earn your trust and your respect, but I will. I will do anything to earn it back."

"What are you going to do about, Arden?"

Torn by loyalty to his sister and his love for Rylee, he knew a sacrifice would have to be made. He made a snap decision. "Rylee, I have to go. I need to see Arden. I need to sort this out—to make it right. Don't give up on me."

He turned and stalked to his car without looking at her. He couldn't bear to see the anguish in her eyes—the uncertainty, the anger or the contempt. Suddenly he knew what he had to do. No matter how painful the results, he knew it was time to publically renounce his sister and withdraw his support of her campaign to gain qualification for the Olympics. He had to clear his name of the doping charge. Maybe then he could face Rylee and dare ask her to share his life.

Her words echoed around and around in his head — *'I don't know if I can ever trust you'*. He knew with absolute certainty that if he didn't have Rylee's trust, he had nothing. His meaning in life would be shattered.

Rylee watched him go—watched the man she loved walk away. Despite what had happened today, she wasn't sure Ash had the strength to make a clean break with his sister. She suspected Arden would talk him around as she had in the past. And if Arden did win her brother over, Rylee knew it would be the end of her and Ash. Her heart spasmed painfully as if it was being ripped in two at the thought, but it was a matter of sanity and survival—hers. Much as she loved Ash, she was not prepared to compromise her integrity and she could not trap herself into some half-life of furtive sex with no future.

And although her decision sliced through her, she knew it was probably for the best if Ash didn't come back, because then she would have to tell him she killed her little brother. She must have whimpered out loud for she felt Regan's hand on her shoulder.

"Rylee don't give up. He said he was going to make it right."

She looked up at her brother. "Yes, right for Arden probably and that will be the end of it for us and it hurts like hell, Regan."

* * * *

Damn damn damn. How the hell do I make this right for everyone? The reality of his situation slammed into him—he couldn't. Someone had to be the loser and he was the one to decide who. Despite his fury at Arden, he still loved her, but to do right by Arden was to betray Rylee's love and his own. He didn't know what he was going to say to his sister. How did one destroy a person's dream?

The thundering blast of a truck horn snapped him back to reality. He registered that he had drifted into the adjacent lane. He swerved back into his own, clutching the steering wheel in a white-knuckled grip. He eased his foot from the accelerator. The car slowed dramatically until it was traveling within the legal limit. The truck roared past with another disapproving blast of the horn. Ash shuddered and concentrated on his driving.

The house was deserted, so Ash drove on to the stables. The only light showing was a faint glow from the storage rooms at the end of a long row of stalls. He walked slowly past the stalls and several horses popped their heads out in the hope someone was bringing more food. Shamal of the Desert, his newest purchase for Arden, snorted and threw his head up and down. Ash sighed. He was a good horse, probably already ruined by his sister.

Ash found Arden in the storage room. He stood unnoticed in the doorway for a moment watching her as she emptied the contents of one cupboard into a large trunk.

"So, Arden, *you're* hiding the evidence."

She started and looked up, her expression distorted with guilt.

"No, I'm— I'm just tidying up," she stuttered, trying to simultaneously slam the other cupboard and the trunk shut.

Ash shook his head. "No you don't."

He strode across the intervening space and stepped between her and the cupboard. He wrenched open the door and felt sick. It was stacked full of bottles, hypodermics, boots with spurs and whips and other bits and pieces he didn't even want to identify. The hurt of her lies hit him in the stomach like a well thrown right hand punch. His breath cramped in his chest as he stared in horror at Arden's chamber of torture equipment.

"My God. How could you do this? I have given you the best facilities, the best horses, plenty of money and my equestrian career. Why?" Ash pointed at the offending equipment.

Arden crossed her arms over her body and glared at him. "Why, big brother? You ask why? Well I will tell you. I have no talent, that's why. I have no affinity with horses. I have no natural ability. The only way I could achieve is to use these aids to force the horses to achieve."

He turned, sorry for her for a brief moment knowing it must be devastating to have to face the fact she was not suited to her chosen sport or craft... To dream an impossible dream and to know she would never be good enough to achieve it.

"Arden..."

He started to soothe her angst, but she cut him off.

"Don't give me platitudes. I know what I am. Rylee has more talent and natural ability in her little finger than I have in my whole body. I was so jealous. I knew even back then. I knew. I doped her horse to make it docile and doped mine to make it hyper because I wanted to win, so badly and there was no other way to achieve it."

"Why didn't you give up?" Ash asked.

His sister sniffed. "I don't know. I just wanted to be good at something. Our stepmother always said I was a failure and now she's been proved right."

"This failure is of your own making," Ash said quietly.

"I know," she muttered as she hung her head.

A flash of sympathy flickered through him. He pushed it away. Now was not the time for sympathy.

"You know I can't support you anymore."

"I know. You love Rylee," she replied her response tight and sharp.

"I love you too. You're my sister. Despite that, I don't like what you have done."

"What will happen to me, Ash?" she asked. "Are you going to take the stables and horses away from me?"

Ash swallowed with a dry constricted throat, reluctant to say what had to be said. "Yes I'm going to take them from you because otherwise you'll continue to destroy perfectly good horses. Then you'll be on your own. I'll also be making a public statement to the effect that I no longer support you because of your methods."

"Please don't. I'll never compete again. They'll force me out."

"That may be so. It's the price you'll have to pay."

"Please don't make it public, Ash. Please."

"I'm sorry, Arden. I have to clear my name and restore my reputation."

"For Rylee?" Arden asked.

Ash nodded. "Yes, for Rylee, but also for Lilli. She needs to know I do not support cruelty to animals and she needs to trust that I will *not* turn a blind eye to it or condone it."

"Damn you, Ash. Damn you." She bent and snatched up a girth from the trunk and charged at him, the length of leather swinging above her head, the buckles clinking ominously as she aimed at his face. The sharp metal spikes stung as they grazed his cheek, but before she could withdraw to swing again, he caught it in a tightly clenched fist. With brutal roughness, he pulled his sister to him. He saw the fear in her eyes as she stared up at him, but the fear was shadowed by defiance and his rage exploded, almost annihilating any affection he still held for her.

"It's over, sister dear. Don't *ever* come near me or mine again," he snarled in her face.

"Ash..." Her wail bounced around the small room. He saw tears in her eyes, but shut himself off from her appeal.

"It's over."

"No, you will not ruin me. You will *not*," Arden screamed and charged at him with a shovel raised above her head.

Ash watched her come. Given Arden was prone to displays of temper that cooled as quickly as they had begun he didn't really believe she would actually attack him. Shocked out of complacency when she kept coming, he ducked to the side, tripped on the girth and fell with a thud. As he tried to scrabble out of her reach, he saw the shovel swinging down and it was too late to move out of the way. A savage pain ripped through him as he staggered under the blow. The world spun in a giddy circle and he fell to his knees. He peered up at his sister. She scowled down at him. Then her face faded, and blackness enveloped him.

* * * *

Ash stirred then stilled as his head exploded into agonizing pain. He opened his eyes. It was dark and he struggled to remember where he was. The smell of horse assailed him. He heard them shuffling restlessly on the other side of the wall. When his vision steadied, he lifted his head with extreme caution and scanned the room. The world immediately spun in an ever increasing spiral. He shut his eyes for a moment then opened them again. The room steadied. He put his hand to his head and tenderly touched the sore spot. He found a large blob of cold stickiness. His fingers were covered in blood.

Then the memory returned of Arden smacking him over the head with the shovel. He glanced around. He was alone. She had left him there to...to what—die maybe? His baby sister, the one he had cared for and protected from the *evil* stepmother and life's little battles, had hit him and left him injured and alone. Something inside him died in that moment and the knowledge that replaced it was painful. He had been strung along by his own sister, probably for most of his life. He knew now he'd been a fool falling for her easy manipulation of his brotherly love. He had lost ten years of love with Rylee and was just about to lose it again. Maybe he had already. She'd said she couldn't trust him anymore. The pain in his chest was almost as real as the pain in his skull. *God damn it. I've been a bloody fool.*

With extreme care he climbed to his feet. He struggled to stand, grabbing for the wall to prevent himself from falling. The room spun and the floor seemed to tilt and slant under his feet. He wobbled and nearly lost his balance again as he pulled out his phone. His vision blurred as he tried to dial—his fingers refusing to go where his brain directed them. He stabbed at the buttons and finally managed to dial the emergency number. Struggling to stay conscious he then dialed his father's number.

"Dad, its Ash. I'm at the stables. I've called an ambulance. Arden has bashed me over the head. I feel pretty crook," he stuttered into the phone.

"Good God, son, are you serious?" his father shouted in the phone.

"Yes and I'm in a pretty bad way," he replied, his words slurred a bit as he fought to stay conscious.

"Take it easy, son. I'm on my way."

The phone slipped from numb fingers and his knees sagged beneath him. He fought the blackness as he collapsed on the concrete floor.

He heard the ambulance screaming into the yard before his father arrived.

"I'm here. Help. I'm here in the storage room," he cried out.

He heard the thud of feet and was vaguely aware of two people in green bending over him. He groaned and tried to get up, but gentle hands pushed him down and murmured reassuring words. Unable to stay alert any longer, he willingly gave himself up to the care of the paramedics.

* * * *

They say you can die from a broken heart. Rylee fought through the vagueness that enveloped her, the pain in her chest almost physical, and she wondered if her heart had actually broken. Lethargy held her in the bed. Outside her window there were plenty of indications that life went on. She could hear the birds singing, the sound of hooves clattering in the stable yard and children's voices shouting. *Thank God for Regan.*

She rolled over and instinctively reached for her phone on the bedside table, but her fingers found empty space. *Damn, what did I do with that? Must have left it somewhere. Probably better anyway. No need to confront the silence from Ash.* A huge emptiness inside blocked her emotions and she lay there numbly. *Need to get my shit together. Move past this pain. Gotta get on with my life – without Ash.*

"Come on, you. Stop wallowing. The world is awaiting your input," Regan said.

Without lifting the pillow off her head, Rylee muttered, "All right, all right, I'm getting there. Bugger off, little brother, and I'll get up, okay?"

"Good—and about time. Hurry up. I have pizza coming," he replied.

"Who gave you permission to be so cheerful when I'm suffering here?"

He ripped the pillow out of her grip and off her head. "Stop whining, sis. I've allowed you to wallow for more than twenty-four hours. Twenty-four hours is good. More is pure indulgence."

"Fine, you big bully. Give me five and I'll be down," she grumbled

"That's more like it. No good Irish woman lets the world defeat her."

Rylee opened her eyes and glared balefully up at her cheerful brother.

"Out, now," he said with a sharp arc of his finger indicating the action she needed to take.

Rylee pushed herself into a sitting position and dangled her feet over the side of the bed. Regan promptly put her slippers on. Rylee watched him without saying a word. She knew her brother was hurt, angry and frustrated for her and this showed he cared. She remembered he had done this for her twice before. First when she had barely been thirteen and they had been preparing for her little brother's funeral—the little brother she had let die. And the second time ten years ago. She'd cried then, for the loss in her life and the grief she held close.

Regan handed her a hanky. "Come now, Ry. Enough of those tears. He isn't worth it."

She sniffed and wiped her nose and eyes. "Regan, you remember when you did this for me before? How you got me on the other side of the pain?"

"Yes, sis, I remember and I'll get you on the other side of this too."

He left then, and she pulled on a jacket and followed him down into the lounge.

As she got comfortable, Regan stood and faced her. "Now, sis, I am about to deliver a few home truths. You won't like it, but I think you need it."

"Really, little brother, and who says you're qualified to deliver them?" Rylee half rose out of her seat.

He grinned and held up his hand. "In the absence of Ma, it's me."

Rylee sank back in her seat. She couldn't argue with that.

"So, you love him?" Regan asked.

Rylee nodded.

"Enough to fight for him?"

Rylee looked down at the floor.

"Damn it. If you don't love him enough to fight for him then maybe you should get over him."

Regan's words tore through her. "I can't get over him, but I've already lost the fight for him. He's gone to Arden."

"Are you sure?"

She hesitated, trying to remember exactly what he had said when he'd left. *'Don't give up on me'* had been his last words. Had she given up on him? Had she stopped believing he could put it right, that he would put her first in this tangled mess? Even if he did, there was Lilli.

"Well?" Regan prompted her.

"But it's not just Arden anymore. What about his daughter?"

"What about her?"

Rylee leaped from the chair. "I can't take on the responsibility for someone else's child. You know that better than anyone. I killed our little brother. Do you think any parent in their right mind is going to let me have responsibility for their child? Even if he turns against Arden—which he won't—he's never going to let me be stepmother to his precious child. And who can blame him? I'm just what my father said, careless and irresponsible..."

Regan stepped forward, grabbed her shoulders and shook her, hard. "Damn it. No, you are *not* what our father says. You are not."

Tears welled up as she threw herself into her brother's embrace. "But I will have to tell Ash. He needs to know. The ultimate decision is his."

"Maybe, sis, but he would be a bloody fool to hold that against you."

She sobbed against his shoulder, her heart clenching in painful spasms. Bitterness, despair and guilt rampaging through her in a maelstrom of emotion.

When Rylee calmed a little, Regan pushed her back into her seat and stood over her, literally, until she had eaten three pieces of pizza and consumed a can of soft drink. She wanted to fight him, but didn't have the strength. In the end the pizza improved her physical well-being and her brother's company helped with the emotional trauma.

"So, what now?"

She shrugged. "I really don't know. He went after Arden. I don't know what it all means. He said he was going to make it right, but I don't know how."

"Sis, he said not to give up on him, remember? Maybe he'll come back."

She shook her head. "It won't do any good, because he has Lilli."

"So?"

"So, brother dearest, despite what you say, all the faith in the world won't make me a responsible stepmother."

"Why not? Just because you can't quite reach the status of angel like our stepmother, doesn't mean you won't do a good job."

She shrugged again. "It's not that. It's Rohan."

Regan gave her a quizzical look. "What about Rohan?"

"What about Rohan?" she shouted. "I killed him. Killed him with my carelessness. How can I ever ask

Ash to let me care for his child, when I've already killed one who wasn't mine?"

"For God's sake, sis. We've been through and through this. You cannot hold yourself responsible for Rohan. You were but thirteen with a house, eleven siblings all younger than you, and Da to care for."

"But I fell asleep, Regan. I fell asleep and Rohan died." Her voice gained volume with each word.

"It's not your fault," Regan insisted.

"Da says it is. He hasn't forgiven me yet," she blurted out.

"Oh, sis, Da is a bitter old man whose own guilt at not doing more at the time to help you keeps him silent on forgiving you," Regan responded sternly.

She dropped her gaze to the floor to hide her tears. "But how can I ever trust myself with another person's child when I failed so dismally. I'm scared of taking that responsibility," she declared.

"Ash loves you and he would be some sort of bastard to hold that against you."

"So does that make our Da a bastard?"

He looked straight at her. "Yup."

"Well it probably doesn't really matter how I feel anyway. Ash has made no attempt to contact me since he left. That sort of speaks for itself. Surely if he was going to out Arden he would have come back and told me."

* * * *

Despite everything, Rylee slept well that night and was ready to face the world the next day—until she reached the stables and saw the St. Wilhelmina's school bus pull up in the car park. The first off the bus was Annie—Lilli, as Rylee now knew her to be.

"Regan, can you take this class. I can't."

"You're even letting that little bugger back on one of your horses?" Regan spluttered as he glared at the child.

Rylee sighed. "Yes. It wasn't her fault. It was Arden's."

"Fine. Which one? Moonbeam is out," her brother observed un-necessarily.

"What about Zea?" Rylee suggested.

He nodded. "Could be a good choice," he commented, with an attempt at a smile. "If the kid tows the line she might be able to go on with her, but I thought her dad wouldn't let her ride."

Rylee shrugged. "Apparently he's had a change of heart. Maybe An... Lilli blackmailed him into it? Who knows?"

"Huh, well she had grounds for it," Regan scoffed before he headed for the stables.

Lilli left the group before they filed into the stables after Regan and ran up to Rylee. "How's Moonbeam?"

"She's healing nicely, but is not ready to be ridden. Besides, I wasn't expecting you to come back," Rylee replied, her tone sharper than she'd planned.

The child's face crumpled. "You don't want me to come back?" she whimpered.

Rylee smiled. "I didn't say that, Ann...Lilli, but your father made it very clear you're not to ride."

"Oh, now he says I can—here with you. He sent a letter because he couldn't come himself. He's in the hospital."

Anxiety clenched Rylee's stomach and her heart paused then beat faster. "Hospital? Why? How?"

Lilli gazed up at Rylee, her eyes filled with tears. "Aunty Arden bashed him with a shovel. He has a bad concussion."

Rylee's jaw sagged. "Arden hit him…with a shovel?"

"She was mad because Daddy told her off about the horses."

"I see," Rylee said softly. It must have been a pretty nasty confrontation if Arden actually assaulted him. Surely Ash would not be so forgiving after that. Perhaps there was hope yet for their love. "Well, you go and visit with Moonbeam while I read your father's letter and speak with Ms. Winters."

"All right." Lilli headed into the stables.

Slowly Rylee tore the envelope open, almost too afraid to read the letter inside. The paper crackled between trembling fingers.

My dearest Rylee,
Lilli will no doubt inform you I am in hospital. I have tried to call you, but all my calls remain unanswered. I will assume that this means you no longer want to see me and I will try my hardest to respect your wishes.

He had been trying to call her. Oh hell, she hadn't seen her phone since that night. She had been too miserable to even miss it. *Damn.* She went on reading.

But Lilli has expressed a clear desire to ride – and ride at your stables – and you are the one person other than myself I trust to teach her. I request that despite our differences, you will take Lilli under your more than capable wing and teach her to ride well. There will be no more incidents of abuse of your horses by my child. Lilli is more than aware now of right and wrong.
Ms. Winters has my instructions in writing also, so I don't expect any trouble from her or the school.

I'm sorry that we could not resolve our differences. I will love you for the rest of my life and I hope you find what it is you seek in the future.

Love,

Ash

Rylee screwed the letter up and shoved it into her pocket. Her throat was so constricted she could hardly speak as she confirmed with Ms. Winters that Lilli could ride then went to the stables to find Ash's child. If she stopped to think now, she would sink right back into her pit of despair. Instead she prepared Zea and introduced the child to the horse.

"My gosh, Zea is so big," Lilli gasped.

Rylee laughed. "She is, but she is also gentle and well educated. If you treat her right, I believe you two will suit each other well. The rules of course are—no aids unless approved by me, no rough handling and definitely no riding unsupervised until I say so." She squatted down and looked directly into the child's eyes—eyes so much like Ash's that for a moment Rylee was disorientated. She focused. "Promise me, Lilli."

Lilli stared directly back at her. "I promise. I've learnt my lesson. I'll always do what you say."

Rylee kept Lilli separate from the rest of the class, working on basic skills and letting the horse and rider get accustomed to each other. Lilli followed her every instruction to the letter, and Rylee had relaxed a little by the end of the lesson.

When the children climbed back in the bus for the return trip to school, Rylee turned to Regan. "Where's my phone, little brother?"

"Oh, I put it in the desk drawer, the right one. Been feeling it's absence, have we?" he asked with a chuckle.

She grimaced. "Apparently Ash is in hospital and has been trying to ring me."

"What?"

"According to Lilli Arden beat him up, but he now thinks I don't want anything more to do with him."

"And?"

"Oh for God's sake, Regan, I don't know. Okay, I just don't know anything right now, except that I love him."

"Well go, sis. Go and see him. Talk to him. For goodness sake, sort out your differences and I can get off this rollercoaster ride."

"You get off?" Rylee exclaimed.

"Yes, dear sister, unrequited love's peripheral victims. I'm one of them."

Rylee laughed then and danced all the way to the house to find her phone.

Chapter Eight

When Rylee entered the ward, she was shocked to see the bruising and cuts to Ash's face. He was pale and appeared to be totally miserable until he turned and saw her hovering in the doorway. His face lit up and his mouth curved up into a very kissable smile.

"You've come," he said.

She grinned. "Of course. I had to come and see you were all right. I didn't answer my phone because my brother switched it off and hid it."

Ash chuckled. "He hid it so this bastard couldn't hurt you anymore, I'm sure."

She slipped into the chair by the bed. "Maybe."

"I won't hurt you anymore. I promise."

"And Arden?" she asked.

Ash frowned. "I'm no longer associated with Arden. I have given my publicity department instructions to issue a media release publicly disowning my sister and distancing me from her practices and to send letters to all the appropriate bodies. I've also included a statement absolving myself from the doping incident and explaining my reasons for taking the blame in the first place. I don't know what the fallout will be for me, but I know my sister's equestrian ambitions will be destroyed."

"That must have been so difficult for you. I know Arden deserved it, but she is your sister."

"Yes, but I didn't deserve this either. I think she's gone a little mad with the constant struggle to achieve something that's out of her reach."

"Perhaps. At least it's no longer looming between us."

The nurse came around to shoo people out of the ward so Ash took her hand before she could leave and pressed a kiss on the back of her hand. "Take this for now, and when I'm out of here, I am going to fuck you to within an inch of insanity and love you with all my heart. Don't say you haven't been warned."

She leaned into him and whispered, "I'll be waiting."

* * * *

Each night she visited Ash in the hospital and they talked — *really* talked for the first time since the doping incident — he about his sister's terrible relationship with his stepmother, Ruth, and how she had led him to believe Ruth was cruel to her and how he had protected and continued to protect her. They filled in the missing ten years and fully digested the doping incident.

On the third night of visiting the hospital, Rylee drove up to the stables happy about the way things were heading. It was raining heavily, but she could see something was wrong. Open stable doors were creaking in the wind — doors that should have been closed. She jumped out of the car and checked the stables. They were empty. She ran to the house, but it was shrouded in darkness. She pulled on her weather proof jacket and rubber boots, grabbed the big torch by the door and set out. The horses couldn't have gone far. She was convinced Arden was to blame. She walked, the wet grass slapping at her legs, the rubber boots dragging at her feet. A gray shape loomed up out of the rain. The mare, Rainbow Cloud, stood with her back to the wind and rain, her tiny foal huddled under her belly. The horse snorted when Rylee appeared but didn't move away. She grabbed the halter and urged the horse forward. It didn't take long for her to return them to their stall. She filled her deep pockets with oats and a couple of lead ropes then turned immediately and headed out once more into the storm. She knew horses could stand up to extremes in weather, but her horses were used to warm lodgings and none of them had coats on. But the thing that worried her most was that the highway ran down one side of her property and the creek down another, both of which would prove dangerous for her horses on a night like this. She neared a stand of trees. She heard one nicker of greeting then several nickers as Moonbeam trotted to meet her. She gave the pony a handful of oats and suddenly she was surrounded by six hungry ponies, the dun horse, Zea, and the huge looming bulk of Monti. She gave oats out all round. With oats on offer, Rylee knew the ponies would follow her back to the stables, so she clipped leads on Monti and Zea and headed back. As she expected, the six ponies trailed behind Monti and Zea. When she reached the stables, she found Shannon standing in the yard, half his body in the stable the other half out in the rain. She smiled. *Trust the old boy to come home.*

She stabled all but Shannon then left a note for her brother and the stable lights on, knowing he would investigate when his mate Andrew brought him home from the pub. She saddled up Shannon and set out again. She had two to find—Lord Thornleigh and Boomerang Joe. She shivered with the cold, but the burning anger and resentment heated her core. The wind tugged and ripped at her. Shannon lowered his head and picked his way carefully. Rylee knew he would much rather be in his warm, dry stable. She heard hooves above the whistle of the wind. Shannon nickered, then snorted and whinnied when Lord Thornley came up behind and nipped his rump. Rylee turned Shannon and quietly put her hand out to secure the big hunter's halter. Thor made a half-hearted effort to pull away, but when she moved forward, he followed. Andrew's car was in the yard when she arrived and she felt a rush of appreciation for the bloke who drove her brother everywhere at night. Regan never talked about his night blindness and the shame he felt about his affliction.

She dismounted and walked the two wet horses inside. Regan had stripped down to his singlet for the task of brushing and drying horses. Andrew, a strict non-animal person, was perched on a bale of hay watching. Rylee could smell warm mash, wet horse and rain.

"Oh, Regan, thank goodness you're here," she said, turning the two horses into their stalls then sinking down on the nearest bale of hay.

"You all right, sis? What the hell happened?" he demanded to know.

"I'm not sure, but when I arrived home, all the stables were open and the horses gone. I'm still missing Boomer. I'm going out again."

* * * *

It was almost dawn when she returned without Boomerang Joe. She had found gates open into neighboring properties and to the highway. She was desperately afraid for the horse she had come to love.

She was huddled in front of the fire drinking hot chocolate when Regan came in. He went straight upstairs and had a shower. When he came back, he flopped on the lounge beside her.

"No Boomerang?"

She shook her head. "All the gates were open. He could be anywhere. As soon as it's light, I'll go out again. And could you call all the neighbors then go out along the highway."

"Sure, Ry. Don't worry. We'll find him."

"I hope so. I've come to like the big boy. I've even thought of doing some competitive endurance — perhaps eventually the Tom Quilty. It's far enough removed from eventing not to have bad memories for me."

"Great, sis," Regan said smiling. "So how are things with, Ash?"

She nodded. "Good, although I think he is struggling to accept how things have turned out with Arden."

"And have you told him?"

"Told him what?"

"Why you are afraid to be a stepmother to his child?" Regan replied.

She shook her head.

"You have to tell him, Ry," Regan warned.

"Yes, I do have to tell him that my carelessness killed my baby brother."

"No, damn it. Tell him your fears, so you can have a relationship, so you can be a mother to Lilli — so he'll understand your cautiousness," Regan grumbled at her.

"Oh for goodness sake, let me have a few weeks of pleasure before it has to end," Rylee protested.

"It doesn't have to end."

"Of course it does, little brother." Rylee sighed deeply. "Would you let your child be mothered by a woman who has already killed a child? Well, would you?"

"Ry, it wasn't like that," Regan said.

"Well, you explain it. You were old enough to remember." She stormed off up to her room.

* * * *

Two days later, Ash was discharged from the hospital and he immediately headed out to see Rylee. The place seemed deserted, but after a quick search around, he heard her singing and rattling around in the loft. He climbed the ladder and found her folding cotton rugs and saddle blankets. She hadn't heard him arrive and he stood there on the top rung of the ladder watching her. Her lithe body was encased in clinging jodhpurs and a dark tight singlet top with a low neck, showing a long indentation of cleavage. Her dark curls bounced with her movement, hiding her face as she bent over displaying her curvy little butt right in front of him. His groin ached, but a tiny edge of apprehension tickled at him. Had he done enough to make it right between him and this sexy desirable woman? Would she welcome his loving? They had talked of many things in the hospital and while he liked to think it was all sorted, he didn't think he could bear her rejection right now.

He climbed the last rung, tiptoed up behind her and grabbed her around the waist, pulling her butt hard against his swollen groin.

"Ekkkkk."

"I've come to claim my woman. Will she have me?"

Rylee spun around in his arms and glowered up at him. "You scared the heck out of me."

He tucked his hands under her butt and pressed her against him. "Sorry. Didn't mean to frighten you, but my animal instincts got the better of me when you were waving your little butt in my face."

"You cheeky bugger," she responded, pressing herself against his hardness. "And what animal instincts would those be?"

"Do I really need to explain?"

"No."

She wriggled her body against his.

"Then will you have me, woman? I want to fuck you until we are both so spent we'll be sleeping here in the loft."

"Yes, I'll have you."

"Now?"

"Mmmm, yes, now," she murmured.

He showered light kisses over her cheeks, eyes and neck before he lowered her to the rugs on the floor. He covered her feminine curves with his body and entwined his long legs with hers.

With deliberate slowness he undid each button on her shirt, kissing every inch of flesh as he uncovered it. Her breasts rose above the edge of her lacy bra and her nipples were firm little peaks straining against the flimsy lace. With one large hand, he slid the material aside and lowered his head to suck at her dark nubs of erect flesh. Expertly he unclipped her bra and lifted it out of the way before moving to her other breast and running the tip of his tongue around her areola. Then he moved down to finish undoing the buttons on her shirt before he pulled the two pieces of material apart exposing her upper body. He returned to plant a trail of tender kisses over the soft swell of her tits before he moved with deliberate slowness down her rib cage across her abdomen before pausing at her navel. Here he dipped his tongue into the shallow indentation before running it around the rim and dipping it in again. "Rylee, my love. So gorgeous, sexy and all mine."

She reached up and tousled his short hair before grasping it tightly and pulling him down to her. She stretched up and kissed him hard and demandingly before giving his head a little push downwards.

He laughed. "And she's impatient too." He obeyed and undid her jodhpurs. A small amount of squirming helped him dispose of them down to her ankles, at least. Then he had to pull away and stand. Rylee lay on her back, unable to hold in the giggles as she watched him struggle to pull her riding boots off and finally remove her jodhpurs. He scowled at her and proceeded to rip his clothes off. Then he pounced on her again, this time with nothing between them. "You're a minx—a shameless minx, Ms. O'Shaughnessy, lying there laughing while you lover struggles with your restrictive clothing. Not even lifting your little finger to help."

"Oh, I thought I was helping," she said with a tiny chuckle. She eased her hand down between them and closed it over his fully erect cock and stroked her hand up and down the smooth throbbing shaft.

"Mmmmmm."

"Is that helping?"

"Oh very much so," Ash moaned against her skin.

He brought his hand between her legs and delved into the wetness between her legs. "How about this?" he asked.

"A little," she hummed, moving slightly to accommodate his access.

He kissed her, nibbling and exploring her mouth inside and out while he moved his fingers with ever increasing firmness around her entrance and over her clit. Her pussy tingled and she whimpered when he dipped his digits inside, probing and caressing. She opened her legs for him, and he lifted himself over her, supporting himself easily while he lowered his head to kiss her. She moved her hand down and guided his penis to the entrance of her pussy. He hovered there for a short while, the head of his cock lying just inside her entrance, enjoying the firmness of her grip on his shaft. He slipped his cock in a little more then withdrew it. He watched for her reaction as he repeated the teasing action again and again.

"Ash, don't tease. Just fuck me. I want you," she cried.

He chuckled and continued his teasing little dance. Rylee lifted her hips to get deeper penetration, but Ash was ready for it, playfully refusing to satisfy her aching need to have him enter her and thrust hard and fast. She cried out in frustration.

He chuckled again. "You really want me?"

"For goodness sake, yes. I want *all* of you."

"Like this?" he asked and sank the full length of his throbbing shaft into her. Every inch of it.

"Yes." She almost screamed with relief and arousal as the single thrust of his cock ignited all the trembling nerve endings into a frenzy. Every bit of her tingled between her legs, down her inner thighs and right up inside her pussy to her cervix. She whimpered her protest when he almost pulled out, but before she could draw breath to protest his withdrawal, he sank all the way in again. Her legs trembled and her climax spiraled from where he thrust into her, through her body to her hair roots and back again. She curled her toes under the intensity and groaned her pleasure as she reveled in the sensation of Ash's continued slow thrusting. She dragged in a deep breath and stilled while the vibrations of his climax throbbed and reverberated on the now sensitive walls of her pussy. Then he sagged onto her, his penis still embedded inside her body. He lay for a long moment, his chest heaving as he tried to catch his breath. Then he rolled off her, taking her and the horse blanket with him. She laid her cheek on his chest and softly stroked his skin. He ran his hand idly over her hair as they remained joined for a long moment. Every cell of her body was relaxed—content. She sighed and kissed his jawline as she felt him slip out of her. Still they didn't move, but clung together for a long time in their private cocoon, the sound of horses snuffling and stamping below the only thing that intruded into their golden afterglow. Rylee wanted to preserve this feeling between them forever.

The light had faded before either of them moved. Reluctantly Rylee crawled out from under the rug and pulled on her clothes.

She knew these trysts would have to end soon. She couldn't bear to tell Ash that her carelessness had killed her baby brother. She couldn't bear the thought of seeing uncertainty and fear in his eyes when she looked after Lilli—the blame she had seen for years in her father's. She never wanted to see that look in Ash's eyes. She would rather never see him again than have to carry that in her memory until the end of her days.

* * * *

The rain thrummed steadily on the roof. Both Regan and Ash were seated in front of the fire, sipping hot chocolate and eating hot buttered toast while plates of thick homemade soup cooled in chunky pottery mugs. Rylee was suddenly overcome with shyness under her brother's probing gaze with the feel of Ash's loving still warm on her skin. She lowered herself into the chair closest to the fire and stretched her hands out to the flames.

"You ok, sis?"

"I'm fine, you two. Stop fussing."

Ash cleared his throat. "I saw Arden this morning. We've talked about the future." He touched his bruised face. "I talked, she cried and made excuses, but nothing is going to change my mind. I realize I've been an idiot—like an ostrich, burying my head in the sand. I didn't want to see what Arden was doing. I didn't want to stop loving my sister."

"Ash—" Rylee began.

He put his finger to her lips. "Shhh, just listen. I need to get this out before it drives me insane with guilt and rage."

She sat and clasped her hands in her lap. She hungered for the man in front of her. He appeared so anguished and beaten, but underneath she could sense a band of determination. She desperately wanted to take him into her arms, but he warded her off and she sank back into her seat.

"I made the wrong choice ten years ago, but I'm not going to make the same mistake again. Arden has made her own destiny and if she doesn't like it, there is nothing I can do about it. My future is with you, if you'll have me."

She leaped out of her chair and flung herself into his embrace. "Oh, Ash, I do love you."

He hugged her tightly, but then pushed her away. "I know you love me, Rylee. I've never doubted that, but I need you to respect and trust me too. Can you?"

"I want to. Today...fronting up to Arden, admitting you turned a blind eye and refusing to continue condoning her behavior has been a big step. I know this has been incredibly painful for you, but I don't expect it's finished yet. I respect you for taking this step, but can you stand by your decision when Arden comes crying or when the media take a stab at her. Will you be able to put us first? I need to know that. I need to be sure you won't renege on your decision— that you will never support or ignore her wrong doing again."

"I know, and it's what you deserve. It's what I want to give you. I know my words will never be enough. Just give me time, my love. I need a chance to show you I can be trusted."

She sank to her knees in front of him. "I love you, Ash. I know you love your sister, despite her behavior. I'm not asking you to reject her so completely, just her behavior. I know it's going to be heartbreaking, but I'll stand by you. We can do this together."

He cupped her face and placed a chaste kiss on her mouth. "And Lilli..."

Her own fear snatched at her happiness in that moment. Ash may have repaired his bridges and declared his love and loyalty, but she was yet to reveal her tragic secret, and that revelation could change it all. Ash must have sensed her hesitation. He let his hands drop to his lap. "Rylee?"

She knew he was asking if she was willing to make the arrangement a family. She couldn't bring herself to end it right now. Rylee looked across at her brother. He frowned at her and nodded. She knew he was trying to indicate that this was her moment to tell. The words choked in her throat. She couldn't do it. Instead she said, "Yes, and Lilli."

* * * *

Two days later, Reg called.

"Boomerang Joe has just turned up here, Rylee. He's in bad shape. Looks to me like he's been ridden to within an inch of his life. I've called the vet."

"I'm on my way, Reg," Rylee cried into the phone.

Regan insisted on driving, and Rylee called Ash to cancel their date.

"Boomerang Joe just turned up at Reg's. He's injured."

"I'll meet you there," Ash replied.

* * * *

By the time they arrived Ash was already standing by the horse, his hands clenched into fists at his side while Reg soothed the distressed animal as the vet examined him.

Rylee went to the horse and stroked his forehead. "You poor baby. What happened, big boy? How did you get into such a state?"

The big gray gelding looked sorry for himself as the vet examined him. He had a couple of gashes across his rump—jagged cuts where spurs would connect—across his neck and face, one fetlock was cut and he held one of his back legs off the ground. "Well, in my opinion, he has been ridden to an inch of dropping, spurred on and beaten over the head with a riding crop or whip of some kind. The legs could be from blows or riding hard on rough ground," the vet stated bluntly.

"Bloody hell, who would do this to a horse?" Reg ran a gentle hand over Boomer's rump.

Rylee glanced at Ash, but clamped her mouth shut, not wanting to make the accusation against Arden out loud. She knew the woman had no respect for horses, but to do this to an animal totally out of spite was disgusting even for her. Rylee was gutted to see such a beautiful animal—her animal—with such terrible damage. If Arden had appeared at that moment, Rylee knew she would have beaten the crap out of her, given her some of her own treatment. She paced back and forth, trying to calm her fury before she touched the horse. Tears stung behind her eyes and as she stalked back to the car. She stood there for a long moment then kicked the tires several times until her toe hurt. She stepped back, took a deep breath then returned to the stables. Ash had said nothing as he watched her take her frustration out on the expensive rubber of his wheels, had just stood there observing the injured horse and shaking his head.

"Boomer old fella, we'll fix you," she murmured as she stroked his neck and chest.

The big horse snuffled at her hair and moved restlessly. "I know who would do this." Ash frowned.

"For revenge," he snarled. "Do you want to report her to the RSPCA, or I can deal with it, Rylee?"

She shook her head. "Let it go, Ash. I think we have enough between us without me sending your sister to prison."

Everyone stood in stunned silence as Ash dialed and waited. No answer.

"I'll deal with it, and, Damien, I'll also deal with the vet bills. Spare no cost. He's a good horse."

"Sure. He should repair okay. Just the knee I'm worried about and I wouldn't move him for a while."

"No probs. Boomer can stay here for as long as needed," Reg said.

"Good, give me the bill, for board and food," Ash replied.

"I will and what about Cockatoo Ridge? I don't want one of mine in her hands."

"Don't worry. All the horses are under the care of a temporary manager. I have plans for their future that don't include Arden."

Reg nodded. "Right."

"You sure you don't want to report her, Rylee?" Ash asked.

"No, not this time," she said.

* * * *

The phone rang early Monday morning. Still eating breakfast after mucking out the stables, she snatched up the phone. "Rylee," she mumbled through a mouthful of toast.

"Hi, it's Lilli here. I'm on holidays now and I would like to come for a riding lesson. Dad says he can bring me. He said he'll bring a picnic and we could all go riding together."

"Oh hi. Of course you and your dad can come. What time?"

"He said about eleven."

"Okay, see you then."

Rylee sank back in her chair. She had been terrified Lilli would demand to come riding by herself. She had spent the last couple of days thinking up suitable excuses for why she couldn't accommodate the child.

She hadn't seen Ash since the episode with Boomerang Joe. She missed him, but work demands had kept him holed up as he tried to clear his schedule to be available for his daughter, now that Arden was out of their lives.

* * * *

Her breath caught in her chest as he stepped out of the car. Every line of his muscular body was emphasized by the black riding breeches, knee high boots and a casual blue button-through shirt that clung snugly to his chest, topped with a black leather bomber jacket. The wind had ruffled his hair and he was smiling as he pulled two saddle bags from the back seat.

Rylee snapped her gaping mouth shut and ran toward him. He draped the saddle bags over his shoulder and held his arms wide. She fell into his embrace and he hugged her close, dropping a light kiss on the tip of her nose.

"Come on. Let's go riding. All that kissing stuff can wait till later." Lilli tugged at Rylee's vest.

She pulled out of Ash's arms, disappointed with the shortness of the greeting. She gave a pretend pout at her lover, and Ash smiled and winked at her, as she allowed Lilli to drag her toward the stables. As they moved away from him, Ash tapped her on the backside. She squeaked and did a little skip out of his reach. He chuckled and lengthened his stride to come up beside her. He promptly tucked his arm around her waist and pulled her against his lean length.

"Can't keep those horses and the kid waiting, you know," Ash said.

Rylee smiled up at him. She knew he was promising more — later.

He leaned close to her ear. "Besides, she's safely in bed by nine," he whispered.

Rylee had already groomed the horses and done their feet so she just pointed out the tack. Although she could manage the bridle because of Zea's size, Lilli needed a little help with the saddle and tightening the girth. As she worked beside her, Rylee quietly advised and instructed the child, reminding her of all the things she needed to do for the safety and comfort for the horse. By the time they had finished, Ash was just doing up the girth on Monti and Thor was already saddled. The three of them walked out of the stable side by side. A wave of emotion washed over Rylee. They might as well have been a family, but they weren't because Lilli wasn't hers and she was terrified of being expected to supervise the child alone. That itself prevented them from ever being a family, just as soon as she got the guts to tell Ash of her failure.

She rechecked and tightened Zea's girth a little — the mare had a habit of puffing up when first saddled. She helped Lilli do up her helmet then held out her hands to give the child a boost onto the fifteen hand horse.

"Up you get, miss," she said.

Lilli bounced into the saddle and once she was settled she, adjusted her feet in the stirrups. She took hold of the reins, just how she had been shown, and while she waited for the adults she stroked Zea's neck.

Rylee smiled. Lilli was a smart kid with a natural talent for riding that she must have inherited from her father. Rylee looked up to find Ash watching them both intently.

"You're so good with her," he said.

Rylee felt sick with guilt and deceit. She wasn't good with children. She couldn't be trusted with their safety. The only thing was Ash didn't know this.

"She's great."

He smiled and offered his cupped hands for a leg up on Thor.

He grinned. "I know you didn't need it. I just wanted to — you know — be close to you."

Rylee laughed. "Shall we go then?"

Regan came out of the shed as they rode past. He waved. "Enjoy the ride."

All three waved to him.

"We will," Rylee shouted back.

Once out of the yards Rylee consulted Lilli. "Are you ready for a canter?"

The child grinned. "Yes. You know this is the first time Dad has seen me ride."

"I saw you..." Ash began but immediately fell silent.

Rylee raised her eyebrows at him and shook her head, glad he had not continued.

"Your father should be proud of how far you've come. Okay, start with a trot. Sit up straight then ask Zea for a canter. Remember, use your right leg behind the girth. And move your bum how I showed you. Okay, you go first."

"Yes," Lilli replied.

Rylee watched as the child went through the motions to ask Zea for a canter. She did fairly well, and Zea obediently led off on her left leg. Zea had a beautiful smooth canter. She looked across at Ash watching his child cantering away from them.

"Shall we?"

"Yep."

They moved forward together.

Rylee thought her heart would burst as they cantered across the paddock with the wind in her face, the sun warming her skin and the powerful horse beneath her, carrying her side by side with the man she loved. All her nerve endings tingled as the scents of horse, hay and leather wafted around her, teasing her senses. She glanced at Ash appreciating his athletic body moving as one with the horse, his legs relaxed and hands firmly on the reins. Later tonight they would move as one when he made love to her. She shivered at the thought as sparkles of emotion burst inside her brain. God she loved this man. Then she glanced forward and saw Lilli, secure in her seat, looking every inch the rider her father was and her heart squeezed into a lump, a heavy rock behind her breast. She had become fond of Lilli, enjoyed her company and thrived on teaching her to ride, but at the same time she was terrified of the girl. She couldn't go on lying to Ash for much longer and her heart wrenched with the pain of what her revelation would do. She couldn't bear the thought of Ash glaring at her the way her da had done.

"Shall we go down by the creek for lunch? It appears Lilli is headed that way," Ash shouted to her.

She nodded. They followed Lilli, who had by now slowed to a walk as she negotiated the slope and the trees.

"Shall we stop here?" she called over her shoulder as she brought her horse to a halt.

They reined in beside her and sat for a moment admiring the creek bubbling its way over a bed of rocks. Reeds edged the bank in places, rustling softly in the breeze and nearby a frog croaked. A couple of weeping willows leaned over and shaded the bank to the right. It was grassy and a felled tree trunk provided a perfect seat.

Lilli slipped from the saddle. "Come, you two slow coaches. I'm starving."

Ash jumped down and began to undo Monti's girth. "First things first, young lady. Make Zea comfortable. Can they go free, Rylee?"

She nodded. "This is a fenced paddock and Zea and Monti both come when whistled and Thor will follow."

Lilli obediently unsaddled Zea and put a head collar on before she took her riding boots off, rolled up her jodhpurs then waded into the shallow stream.

She squealed. "It's so cold. Oh heck, it's freezing," she cried, but made no attempt to come out of the water.

Ash laughed at his daughter's antics then grabbed Rylee's hand and pulled her up against him. Rylee realized they were now concealed behind Monti, who had decided to munch on the grass right where he stood. Ash wrapped both hands around her waist and pulled her into a tight embrace. She immediately felt his erection pressing into the softness of her abdomen.

"God, woman, I need you. I want to make love to you so desperately that if Lilli wasn't here, I would take you right here in the grass."

She shivered as he cupped her buttocks with one hand and slid his other up between her legs and began to caress her through the thin material of her jodhpurs. Her body hummed, her pussy clenched and pulsated. While he touched her, he lowered his head and claimed her mouth, firmly, exploring inside and out. Desire exploded at the taste of him, the feel of his hand between her legs. Her knees melted and she almost crumpled, but his hand clutching her buttocks held her upright. She dissolved into a puddle of need, a primeval ache to feel his cock pressing into her. She moaned against his lips and he applied more pressure to her mound. She rubbed against him, the close contact igniting a fiery explosion between her legs that gushed through her body. She whimpered, but he kept his mouth on hers to silence her cries of rapture. As he applied more pressure the fire exploded into a dancing circle of stars, and he held her tightly as she shuddered through her orgasm.

"Mmmm, very enjoyable," he murmured as he nuzzled her neck.

"Ash, oh my God, Ash."

He chuckled. "Oh my God, what? That my daughter is playing in the creek or that I made you come without actually touching you?"

She looked up at him, not sure whether to be scandalized at his behavior or her own.

"Come on, you two. Stop being all mushy up there. Bring the lunch. I'm hungry."

"We're coming, Miss Muffet," Ash shouted back.

As Ash pulled the saddle bags off Monti, Lilli climbed out of the water, but she didn't replace her boots.

Rylee spread the blanket out by the log and sat on the ground with her back resting against it. Ash placed the saddle bags beside her and squatted on the other side of them. Lilli plonked herself down between their feet, forming a cozy little circle.

Ash had packed sandwiches and cocktail sausage rolls, fruit and cute little pink cupcakes that Lilli promptly informed her they had made together.

"Really?" Rylee exclaimed and looked at Ash.

He smiled as his face flushed a delicate pink. "Lilli and I have been cooking together since she was about three. I have become a dab hand at cupcakes and her other love, lasagna."

"Well I'm impressed."

"And so you should be, Miss O'Shaughnessy."

Between the three of them, they demolished almost all the food and the bottles of icy cold juice. It was perfect. Rylee could have quite easily laid back and snoozed. She was sated and content, but Lilli wasn't about to let her alone.

"So, Rylee, do you like my dad?" she asked.

Rylee shot a momentary glance at Ash, seeking guidance. He just smiled at her, making it clear he was leaving her to sink or swim and that he was just as interested in her answer as Lilli was.

Rylee cleared her throat. "Yes, I do like your dad."

"Do you like me?" Lilli asked.

Rylee shivered. This was getting too close to her secret. Of course she liked the kid, but she damn well didn't want to take responsibility for her on her own. She met Lilli's direct stare with one of her own. "I like you a lot."

"Enough to be my mother?"

Rylee gasped. Lilli's question hit her right in the heart. There was only one way to answer that question — with the truth except for a silent proviso just for her — that she didn't have the kid on her own.

"Yes, sweetie, I like you enough to be your mother, but that role will depend on your dad. If he likes me, warts and all, enough to be his wife."

"But you don't have warts. Only witches have warts."

Rylee stared at the child, stunned by her reply. She didn't have an answer to that. Then Ash started to laugh. He laughed so hard he collapsed onto his back on the blanket. Rylee leaned over him and gave him little slaps to the arms. "It's not funny," she wailed.

"It is," he gasped out between bursts of laughter. He grabbed her arms and dragged her astride him.

She straddled him, not sure whether to kiss him or slap him. She felt the hardness of his cock pressing between her legs and was immediately disorientated by a wave of desire. She was conscious of Lilli beside them.

The child stood. "Well I think you two are so mushy with each other you should be married—and that's my opinion. Now I'm going back to the creek to find frogs."

As Lilli disappeared under the softly waving branches of the willow tree, Ash pulled her down and planted a soft kiss on her mouth. As she broke it off, he smiled.

"Well, do we take the child's advice or not, my love?"

A frisson of uncertainty vibrated through her. She so wanted to say yes. She loved this man, had always loved him. But to marry him meant she could no longer evade being Lilli's sole carer and she had to expose her failure before she could say yes.

At her hesitation, Ash frowned then he smiled a knowing smile. "Don't bother to answer that question, my beloved. I know... You're a woman. You want it done properly, the bended knee, the proposal and the ring... I understand."

"I-I..." She glanced over at where Lilli played at the edge of the water. "Well yes, I would like the whole thing. Do you mind?"

He chuckled again. "Not at all, my darling, as long as you say yes."

She sighed. It gave her more time, but the inevitable was looming. She had to tell him before he bought a ring, before he humbled himself by going down on bended knee, before she had to reveal her dark secret that would have him quickly changing his mind.

"Come on. Time to get back. I have lessons later and I want to go over and see Boomerang." Rylee swung herself off Ash's crotch and was glad Lilli was preoccupied, because her father's arousal was pretty evident. He reached down and adjusted his pants. "Damn uncomfortable with a hard-on, my love. I want to stay the night and love you. Do you have room for Lilli?"

Rylee grinned as she climbed to her feet. "Yes, I have a spare bedroom."

He held out his hand. She clasped it and helped him rise. Not that she needed assistance, but it provided another chance for a quick cuddle in his arms. Together they packed the picnic up, and Ash instructed Lilli to get her boots back on because she had to catch her horse.

She did as she'd been told then together they walked to the rise of the gully. Monti was grazing nearby, and Rylee whistled loudly with her fingers in her mouth. Monti lifted his head, neighed shrilly then came at them at a gallop. Moments later Zea and Thor trotted out from behind the gum trees and followed Monti.

"Will you teach me to do that? I want to whistle like that."

"Maybe," Rylee replied.

The child looked a little disappointed at her reply but proceeded to saddle her horse. Ash helped Lilli this time and Rylee watched him go through the steps as she had.

"But I know. Rylee already taught me."

"Listen to your dad, young lady. We all need reminding. You're still young and he is responsible for your safety."

"Okay. I'm listening," she said.

Ash immediately hugged her. "I know Rylee has taught you, love, and she will take good care of you, but well, I'm your dad, and dads worry."

"I know, Dad, especially because of Mummy."

Ash nodded.

It was an intimate moment between father and daughter, and Rylee felt sidelined. *Stupid woman. You don't want that responsibility, damn it. You can't have it both ways.*

They cantered most of the way back but once in sight of the stables, they slowed to walk as Zea was known to get a little eager to get home to food after a long ride.

Rylee's first lesson was waiting when they arrived and she hurried to get ready. Ash and Lilli agreed to take care of the horses, and Ash promised that he would make dinner. As she walked with Monique and Alsia, the new dressage horse, toward the arena, Ash and Lilli whizzed out of the gate.

For almost an hour she instructed horse and rider, working on suppleness, smooth transitions, the rider's seat and the aids. Monique had come on from Pony Club and now wanted to enter a higher standard of competition. Unfortunately, her parents couldn't afford a horse of the standard she deserved so she had come to Rylee. Alsia and Monique had been together for a couple of weeks and seemed suited to each other.

Rylee was aware of his presence before she turned to see Ash standing by the rails. He was studying the horse and Rylee knew his eye for a first class animal was as experienced as hers, if not better. She gave Monique some last instructions then backed up to the fence to observe her ability to follow through the changes they'd agreed on.

"So, what do you think of my new acquisition?" she asked.

He placed his hands through the rails and rested them on her shoulders. "The horse definitely has promise."

"And the rider?"

"Oh she's okay, but I'm more interested in the owner, actually," he whispered in her ear.

"Yes, and you're distracting me."

"All right I'm going. Just wondering how long you were going to be."

"I'm nearly finished here then I want to see Boomerang."

"Fine. I'll drive you."

* * * *

After the meal Lilli was allowed to watch her favorite show then Ash settled her in the upstairs spare room in a T-shirt borrowed from Rylee. Regan was competing in his dart competition at the local pub, leaving them alone.

They sat side by side on the lounge, the television on but ignored.

"Tell me. What do you want for the future? I mean, for this place?"

She got up and retrieved the business plan that she and Regan had put together. She studied his profile as he read the document, but she wasn't thinking about the material he was reading because her head was full of Lilli's childish statement about them being a family. She so wanted to be a family with him and Lilli, but terror from the past haunted her to the point she couldn't see clearly—couldn't see a way to make it happen.

Finally, he looked up. "This is a very detailed plan. The only thing I would like to see is you with more land, perhaps start a stud."

"Unfortunately, that would cost more than I have."

He leaned in and kissed her nose. "I can see that. The other thing is I would like to see you include is a plan for your development as a rider."

"No, Ash, I don't..."

"I know, but what about endurance riding? Why not have a go at the Tom Quilty, not just your clients. Providing Boomerang pulls up okay, he would be the perfect horse. Besides, there is Cockatoo and Shamal."

"But they're Arden's."

"No, they're mine, and when we get married, they'll be yours too—if you want them. Otherwise I'll buy you something else."

"I can't let you do that..." She saw the hurt in his expression and stopped speaking. "Well, maybe we can talk about it—later."

Ash smiled. "Fine with me. I have something better to do and it does not entail talking." He leaned in and took command of her mouth.

Rylee responded with enthusiasm. She didn't want to talk.

She rested her head on the back of the couch, and Ash moved his body until he was almost on her lap.

He kissed her hard and deep, setting off the throb deep inside. Her heart beat in rapid little patters as her skin tingled and sparked under the caress of his fingers brushing her skin. She found his belt buckle and deftly undid it then opened the top button of his pants. He eased himself a little away from her, and she slid her hand between the tight encasing material and his skin. His skin was hot and satin smooth, his cock hard and throbbing. He groaned as she encircled his stiffened shaft.

"I think we should adjourn to your room, before we go too far and get caught with our pants down."

Giggles bubbled up and she squashed them into little snickers as she extracted herself from the firm confinement of his pants, making him groan again with the pressure she deliberately applied on his swollen flesh.

"God, woman, you're putting that right back there ASAP," he mumbled, as he pulled away from her. Using his knees for leverage he pushed himself upright, pulling her with him. Then without another word, he turned the television off, scooped her up in his arms and headed toward her bedroom. Rylee flicked the light switch as they passed.

The curtains were open and the moonlight lay across the bed in a silver pool of soft luminosity. Ash stood her on the edge of the shadows and in the semi-darkness pulled her shirt over her head and undid her pants. When she stood naked, he turned her and pulled her to him. The glow streaming through the window bathed her naked breasts as he fondled her swelling curves. He nuzzled at her neck and shoulder, and she could feel his cock pressing against her back as it strained inside the material. With the flat of his hand, Ash stroked her abdomen and ran his palm over her mound before he brought his hand back up to cup her breast, teasing the nipple with his thumb. She moaned, the sensitive nubs becoming erect under his touch. With his other, he dipped a couple of digits between her lips. She moved her legs slightly apart to allow him access. With the pad of his finger he found her clit, and she gasped at the blaze his caresses ignited. The heat ran like wildfire through her body, sapping her strength. She leaned on him for support. He nibbled at her neck and dipped deeper between her lips until he found the entrance to her pussy. With a whimper for more, she lifted her head, and he nuzzled her neck then nipped her heated skin gently. Her skin sizzled as he sucked and bit, all the time stroking between her legs. The delicious ache in her pussy spread, tingling along her veins through her flesh, pulsing and throbbing. She groaned and whimpered as the fire consumed her. Then she cried out as he plunged his fingers inside her and moved them around vigorously. The world exploded into a dizzying whirl as the pulse of her orgasm peaked and spread through her body. She pushed against his insertion, her pussy clutching and squeezing the digits as he continued to move them inside her.

"Oh my God, Ash," she moaned. Overcome with sated weakness, she sagged against him.

With barely a pause, he lifted her then laid her on the bed. He stood for a moment exploring her nakedness with his gaze. She was glowing with satisfaction but still blushed at his blatant scrutiny. Without taking his eyes off her, he tugged himself free of his clothes. Once naked, he moved out of the darkness.

Rylee sighed as she admired his magnificent frame, every curve and angle accentuated or shadowed by the diffused glow, emphasizing his rugged masculinity. His cock stood out, fully erect, his naked balls hung low between his muscular thighs as he stepped forward and knelt on the bed beside her. He parted her legs to expose her inner lips, and she lay back on the pillows. He shuffled closer and brought his head down. She inhaled sharply at the exquisite pleasure that rushed across her skin as he slid his tongue sensuously back and forth over her clit. She lifted her hips ever so slightly to meet his explorations. As he sucked gently on her erect nub, she struggled to breathe, consumed with a fiery arousal that burst from the embers of her first climax. She closed her eyes and opened her mouth to draw in small puffs of air into her constricted lungs. Her legs trembled and she curled her toes in absolute bliss. Lithely, he moved his body over hers, and she slipped her hand between them and guided his hard length to her opening. He didn't pause at her entrance but thrust deeply inside and moved fast and hard. She moaned and met his energetic thrusts with small lifts of her hips. He kissed her face and neck then stared deep into her eyes. She stared back, clutching him closer, scoring his back with her nails as he plunged again and again into her. Scorching tension held her suspended. Her pussy pulsated and clenched tightly around the hard length of his shaft as it moved inside her.

Sweat beaded his skin and he groaned, "Come, Rylee. I can't wait."

The intensity burst through her and she cried out as her orgasm blistered every nerve ending. She felt Ash sink deep and shudder with his own release. She embraced him tighter, clawing at his skin as if to make him part of her. Ash groaned and collapsed on top of her. She stroked his back and shoulders and ran her fingers through his hair before pulling him to her, claiming his mouth with a passionate caress of her own. As their kiss ended in a lingering touch, he laid his head on her shoulder and eased his weight from her.

They lay entwined, sexually sated and in silence for a long time in the quiet darkness.

Ash nuzzled her neck. "I want to do that every night for the rest of my life and then it won't be enough to make up for the time we've lost."

She pressed her lips to his cheek, fighting a small wave of sadness that tried to consume her.

* * * *

Ash had only been gone for two days, but already Rylee missed him terribly. Lilli was having a sleepover with a friend then going to her grandparents while her father was away. Rylee had breathed a sigh of relief when she'd found out that the arrangements were already in place and no matter how much Lilli's protested, Ash had insisted they stand as arranged. But despite this escape — or perhaps because of it — Rylee was even more conscious of the unpleasant secret snapping at her heels, howling for revelation.

Lilli's first pleading phone call went to the answering machine and Rylee was glad but felt guilty as she listened to the beseeching little voice.

"Rylee, its Lilli. I'm bored here at Grandpa's. There's nothing to do. Could I come riding with you, please?"

Rylee didn't respond. She knew she was a coward, but the thought of having Lilli here to ride without her father or the safeguard of a teacher scared her to death.

Rylee found herself backed into a corner when the phone rang for the second time. She let it go again to the answering machine.

Lilli wanted to come and ride. Panic screamed in Rylee's head. She couldn't do it. She made excuses to herself and knew they sounded lame.

She got caught the third time.

"You didn't call me back. Can I come for a ride with you?"

"Sorry, sweetie, but I have been so busy I forgot to get back to you. Look, we'll make arrangements for riding when your dad gets back, okay?"

"Oh, can't I come over? Dad wouldn't mind. I know he wouldn't."

"I think your dad wanted you to spend time with your grandparents right now. We'll go riding when he's back."

She heard Lilli crying as she hung up the phone. *Damn it, you're a gutless bitch – to hurt a child like that just because you're too scared.*

Regan glared at her over breakfast on the third morning as the phone rang and Lili left another pleading message.

"For Christ's sake, Ry, tell him. Put him and yourself out of your misery. I can't bear it anymore."

"I can't."

"Then end it. God damn it, sis, for my sake if nobody else's," he yelled at her. "All you're doing is hurting yourself, him and that poor, innocent child."

She dashed out of the door and down to the stables where she hurriedly saddled Thor. She had to get away. To think. To come to terms with the end.

As she led him out of the stable, Ash's car roared into the yard. She halted, her heart pounding. This was it. Ash hurried across the yard and pulled her into a tight embrace. He kissed her hard.

"God I have so missed you, Ry." He pulled back looking from her to the horse. "So you going for a ride then? I thought you'd taken Lilli. Where is she?"

"Lilli? She's not here. Isn't she with her grandparents?"

He stared down at her. "No, they said she was picked up by your brother to come for a ride."

Panic squeezed inside her. "It wasn't Regan."

Now Ash grabbed her arms. She saw the terror on his face.

"You mean she's not here with you?"

Rylee shook her head. "No, she's not here."

Ash paced as he shouted and cursed. Three phone calls later, the search was on for the missing Lilli.

Rylee felt sick with fear and guilt. If only she had said yes to Lilli's request.

Ash raged on and on about the dire consequences to the people responsible.

"I'll damn well kill them if they hurt one hair on Lilli's head. No one hurts my child."

Rylee quailed under his rage, glad she wasn't the target and knew with a terrible certainty she never intended to put herself in that situation.

It was getting late. Still Ash paced and raged. He'd yelled at his father and his stepmother on the phone for letting Lilli go with a stranger and he cursed when Arden failed to pick up. Finally, he threw himself into the lounge and sat slumped there. Rylee sat beside him. She clasped his hand. Ash looked at her—his eyes were filled with unshed tears.

"I'll never forgive myself if anything happens to her. I love her so much. How could my father be so stupid to let her go with a stranger? They had responsibility for her. I should have been here."

"Ash, you can't blame yourself and your parents weren't to know. They'd never met Regan and they knew Lilli wanted to come out and ride."

The shrill ring of the phone tore through the subdued atmosphere in the room. Rylee flinched at the sudden demanding interruption, but Regan jumped up from the chair to answer it before she could respond. "Yes, he's here. I'll put him on."

After a minute or two, Ash slammed the phone down. His face was dark—a deep frown furrowed his brow. "Lilli's in the hospital. Apparently Arden got a friend of hers to pick her up from Dad's on the pretext of her coming out here for a ride. God knows what Arden planned. She was drunk as a skunk and they had an accident at the bottom of the freeway. Lilli is in the Women's and Children's. She's unconscious. Arden is in the Royal Adelaide with a dislocated shoulder, a broken leg and cuts and bruises."

"I'll come. In fact, I'll drive," Rylee said.

Ash didn't argue. He just pulled on his coat and strode out of the door in front of her.

He stared straight ahead, ignoring her as she drove through the night. He moved restlessly in his seat.

Rylee clasped his hand and squeezed. "She'll be all right, Ash. You'll see."

He looked at her for a moment and she saw the tortured expression in his eyes, his fear etched deep in his expression. A lump had settled in her stomach. She knew all too well what it was like to fear for a child.

"No thanks to my sister. She could have killed her. Wait until I get hold of her. I'll never forgive her for this. She was pissed, for God's sake—driving pissed. Lilli is my child. No one hurts her."

Rylee cringed. The memory of her father's angry rant as he'd beaten her echoed in her mind right beside Ash's tirade.

* * * *

The hospital was bright and bustling. A young cheerful nurse showed them into a small room off the side of the ward. Lilli seemed so small in the big white bed with tubes and machines attached to her little bare arms, rattling and beeping with essential data output. She had a large white bandage around her head and already blue-purple bruises were forming around her eyes and down her right cheek. One leg was hidden under a square cage and she had another bandage on her left arm, apparently covering a large gash.

Ash leaned over his daughter and stroked her cheek with gentle fingers. His face, drained of color, looked gray and haggard. His eyes glistened with unshed tears and he sagged into the chair by his daughter's bed. His big hand completely covered her little white one where it lay still on the bedcovers.

"God, I'll never forgive myself if anything happens, but I never thought…" He glanced up at Rylee. "I have *always* given my sister the benefit of the doubt and believed her excuses. Now this. Nothing she says can justify this."

The doctor came, and Ash stood to hear his diagnosis. Rylee saw the desperate pleading in his eyes. Pleading for good news.

"Mr. St. Clair, your daughter is very lucky to be here. She should never have been in the front seat of a sports car at all…"

"No, she shouldn't have been. I did not give permission for her to travel in that car or for my sister to take her from her grandparents' house."

"Nevertheless she is very lucky. We've run tests. There is no sign of major trauma to the brain. She has a nasty gash on her arm and lots of bruising — very lucky, considering."

"Do you have any idea when she will regain consciousness?" Ash asked.

"It's impossible to say. It may be an hour, a day or a week. The brain will take what time it needs to heal. I suggest you and your wife go home and get some rest, because when she regains consciousness, she will really need you then." He left them alone with the inert child and the beeping machines.

Occasionally a nurse came quietly and unobtrusively into the room and made her observations before slipping quietly away again.

"Ash, it's two a.m. — there's nothing you can do here. You're barely awake as it is. What if I book a room at the nearest hotel? It's just up the road. Less than ten minutes in the car."

He stared at her for a long moment then nodded.

An hour later they climbed into the pristine hotel bed and into each other's arms. Ash clung to her. They lay in silence and Rylee felt the dampness of his tears on her shoulder.

Chapter Nine

Two days later, Lilli regained consciousness, with all her faculties intact. Rylee joined Ash at his daughter's bedside. Lilli studied them, her little forehead puckered into a deep frown and unshed tears shining in her eyes.

"Rylee, are you still mad at me about Moonbeam?" she asked with a tiny squeaky voice.

"No, sweetheart, I'm not mad at you. Moonbeam is all recovered now."

"Then why didn't you want to let me come and ride?" Lilli asked.

Embarrassment heated Rylee's face. What could she say? She didn't want to lie to the child. She leaned across the bed cautiously and gave the child a light hug. "I'm sorry I said no. It wasn't that I didn't want you to ride. It's just that I was afraid something might happen to you—like this," she said. "You see I'm not very experienced at looking after children."

Tears welled in her eyes. "And you didn't trust me because I hurt Moonbeam?" Lilli whimpered.

"No, I just didn't trust myself, but I need to learn, so perhaps you can help me."

Lilli nodded. "I'll help you, Rylee, if you say so. So does this mean I can come back to the stables and ride Zea?"

Rylee glanced up at Ash, standing so quietly on the other side of the bed. She searched his expression for any hesitation, but saw none as he smiled and nodded.

Rylee turned back to the child. "Yes, if it's okay with your dad."

"Dad says I can ride, but you have to pick the horse for me. He's still cross at Aunty Arden and he has made me promise never to ride her horses or to go driving in her car again."

"Well that's good, sweetheart, because Arden's horses are trained for her and they can be dangerous for anyone else — especially a beginner — to ride them."

"Right, honey. Rylee and I are going to have some dinner now. I will be back tomorrow to see you. You get some rest."

"Will you come?" Lilli asked in a plaintive tone.

Rylee glanced across at Ash. He smiled and nodded. "Perhaps, but I do have to care for the horses."

"Can I come for a visit then — when I get out?" Lilli asked.

Rylee nodded. "Of course, if it's okay with your dad."

"Dad?" she asked.

"When you get out, missy, we will go visit Rylee, but it'll be a while before you are ready to ride again."

"I know, Dad, but I just like the horses..." She quickly glanced up at Rylee then looked directly at her father. "And I like Rylee too," she said.

"Good. We might see some more of Rylee then. What do you think?" Ash asked his daughter with a sneaky sideways peep at Rylee.

Lilli grinned, the smile a light in the bruised starkness of her face. "I'd like that."

Rylee was struggling to smile. Ash's angry response to Arden injuring Lilli had made her even more wary of revealing her secret. And now she had left it so late that both Ash and Lilli had expectations of a future as a family and she knew she could not fulfill those without telling Ash, because if she didn't, someone else would. As a father, Ash had the right to make a choice.

* * * *

That night, in front of a number of television cameras, Arden announced her retirement from the equestrian arena from her hospital bed. In the same interview, she also pleaded with her brother for forgiveness.

As they watched it on television in Lilli's room, the child moved restlessly in the bed.

"Dad, will I ever see Aunty Arden again? I know she was bad, but she did do nice, fun things with me."

Ash looked at Rylee. "So what do I do with that, my love?"

"The decision is up to you, but she is your sister and I think she genuinely loves Lilli in her own way."

"Could you cope if I allowed her to see Lilli on special occasions like birthdays?"

Rylee nodded.

He leaned in and kissed her. "Just remember my loyalty is yours, now and forever."

Again she nodded.

Ash tuned back to his daughter. "I will talk to your aunt, then we'll see. Okay?"

Lilli nodded. "Yes, Dad."

* * * *

It was past visiting hours, but the ward nurse let them into Arden's private room for a brief visit. The lights were dimmed and they could hear her sobbing quietly as they entered.

Ash went to stand by the bed. "Arden, are you up to talking, just for a moment?"

She looked up at him, her face swollen and bruised. She nodded and tried to wipe the tears from her eyes.

"I just wanted to say you've done the right thing, retiring. You'll find something else to do."

Rylee stood back, not really wanting to be there, but knowing that certain things needed to be said.

Arden sniffed and began to cry again. "I'm so sorry. I never meant to hurt Lilli. I love her and you." She looked toward Rylee. "Can, can you forgive me, Rylee? I think I went mad for a while — the thought of losing all I'd worked for."

"Maybe, Arden — in time, maybe," Rylee replied.

"We'll work on forgiveness. Maybe one day, sis."

"Will you ever let me see Lilli again, please? Ash don't cut me out of her life completely. I know Rylee will take my place, but *please*, will you let me see her sometimes."

"I will give it some thought, but I need to calm down a bit first."

"Ash, please. I'm sorry for all I did — ten years ago, the accident, hurting the horses, lying to you. I'll do anything. I'm getting counseling. I don't want to lose the only family I have."

Rylee stepped forward. Ash looked at her. She gave a slight smile. "Arden, you can't expect forgiveness on your say so. You have to show us both that you *will* make amends. Despite everything, Lilli still loves you." She reached out and took Ash's hand in hers and drew him forward. "And your brother still loves you too."

Ash began to shake his head.

"Your brother still loves you," she repeated. "Even though he's hurt and angry right now, and I won't come between you and them because I know what it is like to be refused forgiveness."

Arden sniffed and hiccupped. "Rylee, I'm sorry for everything. If you can just give me a chance—both of you—I'll prove I'm not all bad. I promise."

"Get better, sis. Until you're on your feet, I'll put an allowance in your bank account. I'll not see you on the streets. Get that counseling and we'll see what the future holds."

The tears flooded down her cheeks and she struggled to speak through choking sobs.

"I will and thank you—both of you."

Rylee turned and left the room. Ash was right behind her. He took her hand and they walked up the corridor together.

* * * *

The three of them had a delightful dinner. Lilli had been declared by Ash fit to go back to school the following week, much to Lilli's disgust.

A hot north wind had been gusting all day and as it lulled, the heat intensified and black thunderheads loomed on the horizon as they settled down to a game of Monopoly.

Lilli moved her token and counted. "One, two, three, four, five. Yeah! I'm going to buy Mayfair then you can all pay me rent," Lilli chortled.

The phone rang as Rylee settled the transaction with the child. She heard Ash's raised voice and wondered what the call was about. When he returned, he looked grim. "They have trouble in Melbourne and want me to go and sort it out. I need to fly out tomorrow morning and it'll probably take me a couple of days to fix. Sorry, my love, but dinner is off for tomorrow night."

She smiled. "Never mind. It can't be helped."

"Yeah and there's another problem. Dad's away until next week."

"That's all right. Dad, I can stay with Rylee."

The inevitable situation she had been dancing around for weeks slammed into her chest.

"What do you think, my love? It would be good practice for being her mum."

Rylee was already pushing herself up out of the seat. She shook her head. "No, Ash. I-I...have the stables to look after."

"Awww, I wouldn't be any trouble. I promise," Lilli cried. "Really I won't."

"No, I can't."

"But why? You two get on great. It would be the perfect solution."

She glared at Ash. "No, I can't."

He glared back at her. "Why?"

Tears welled in her eyes. She danced restlessly on the spot, desperate to escape.

"I can't, Ash. You can't trust me with your child, okay? I'm not to be trusted with kids. I killed my baby brother. I won't risk Lilli."

"What? For God's sake what are you blathering about?" Ash spluttered, shaking his head.

Lilli ran up to him and he wrapped his arm around her shoulders. "But you always take good care of me."

Rylee shook her head. "Someone else has always been there, to keep you safe. I'm sorry, but if you only knew, you wouldn't trust me with you daughter. I can't look after her and I can't be her stepmother."

"Stop. Talk to me," Ash pleaded.

But Rylee was beyond discussion. Her heart was ripping in two. There, she had done it — told him.

"Don't you love me?" Lilli cried.

Ash stepped toward her. She backed away. If he touched her, she would be lost.

"What the hell are you raving about?" Ash reached for her again.

Rylee turned and fled, out of the room, down the passage and to her car. She heard Lilli wail.

"Rylee, come back. Please don't go," Lilli shouted.

"Stop. For God's sake, wait a moment," Ash yelled.

She leaped down the steps and dove into her car. Out of the corner of her vision, she saw Ash and Lilli appear on the verandah. She revved the engine and accelerated out of the circular drive, showering gravel behind her.

The heat pressed in on Rylee as she drove recklessly toward home. All she could think of was getting away — to be alone with her failure, her shame and her loss. Not only had she lost the man she loved with all her heart, she had also lost another child — Lilli, the maddening little girl she had grown to love. But this way at least Lilli was safe from her carelessness and Rylee would never be subjected to the rage Ash had turned on his sister after the accident.

* * * *

Regan arrived just as she was leading Thor from the stable.

"What you doing here, sis? I thought you were staying the night with Ash?"

She could barely see Regan through the blur of tears. "I was, but he asked me to babysit Lilli for a couple of days. I couldn't put her at risk so I told him. I told him I killed my little brother and I was not fit to care for kids."

"Did you explain?" Regan asked reaching for the bridle.

"I said what needed to be said," she snapped, pulling Thor's head out of his reach.

"You're a bloody fool, Rylee. A damn bloody fool."

She swung up into the saddle and, after one long look at her brother, she turned the horse and kicked him into a canter.

She had to get away—from the demons that rattled inside her head and away from Regan's voice of reason and the child who wanted her for a mother. Thor was toey at the unexpected exercise and it didn't take much urging for him to break into a gallop. They pelted across the paddock and Rylee let him have his head.

They were soon both sweating in the muggy heat. The light had turned an eerie green-gray as the storm clouds covered the sun. The leaves of the gums rattled and scratched in the breeze racing in front of the storm. The air felt heavy, but not as heavy as Rylee's heart. The storm grumbled in the distance. The wind picked up strength now cold and damp in her face. Clouds built on the horizon, but she didn't care if she got drenched. She needed to cast off the restraints.

She rode, but her mangled thoughts came with her — haunting her, mocking her. The day she had slept at the table and woken to find her brother gone — the pain and humiliation she had suffered at her grief-stricken father's punishment, the ostracism she had continued to suffer from him, even after he'd married again and had had three more sons. Thor's hooves thudded dully on the damp ground, almost matching the thud of unresolved issues in her brain. Thunder rumbled deep in the black clouds now covering the sky and an occasional flash of lightning shone through the darkness. Logic told her she should turn for home. She didn't know how Thor would react to the storm, but she refused to let her sensible self win. She kicked the big horse on, and he went down the gully, across the stream, then went to bound up the other side, but she turned him west toward the gorge. The normally small babbling stream was already deeper than usual and gushing over the moss-covered stones and around the bigger boulders. Thor scrambled and hopped over the rough ground, struggling to find secure footing. Rylee was thrown to one side. She lost her stirrup and had to save herself by clinging to the bridle with one hand and the saddle with the other.

What were you thinking? You weren't thinking. You've become a danger to yourself and others. But then you always were a danger to others. She scolded herself for her foolishness, already seeking a safe place to shelter as the rain pelted down before turning into hailstones, whipped by the gusty wind into stinging bullets of ice. Thor baulked at moving forward and danced against her aids wanting desperately to turn around and put his backside to the weather.

She had come so far up the gully in a vague haze of pain. Both sides now rose steep and straight and there was barely room for Thor to turn around. She suddenly realized she had gotten herself into a very dangerous spot because she wasn't going to make it to the exit by the waterfall. There was already too much water gushing down the narrow stream bed, rising so rapidly it would soon be up to Thor's knees. He was jittery and throwing his head around and snorting. He wanted out of the gully, but for him to turn, she would have to dismount, putting her at risk of being trampled in the maneuver.

She slipped from the saddle and went to Thor's head, firmly tugging on the bridle. He began to swing when a roar enveloped the gully. Rylee looked up. A wall of water, logs, stones and other debris towered above her, rushing down the narrow space. Thor reared, swung away from her and galloped down the gully. Rylee screamed, but any noise she made was drowned out by the rumble and splash of the torrent. She scrambled up the rock face, using branches and tree roots. As the surging flood reached her, she tucked herself behind a couple of solid roots and clung to them. The deluge tugged at her, dragged her clothes and hair, and filled her mouth and eyes with muddy water. She clawed at the tree roots, wound her arms around them. The dirt and rocks behind her dissolved and tumbled away as the worst of the maelstrom rushed past. She gasped for air when she could. Something cracked against her head, her vision blurred but she shook unconsciousness away, afraid she would be swept into the swollen stream and drowned. The roots shuddered and began to pull out of the rock face. Petrified, Rylee prayed they would hold and clung to them. Suddenly, the gushing flash flood was gone, along with most of the stream bed and great gouges out of the rock walls. Rylee dragged wheezing breaths into her lungs, tucked her feet under her and tried to stand. Her legs wouldn't support her. They were trembling so much. She peered along the gully, hoping Thor had made it to safety. She sagged back down and sat in the mud, not sure what to do next.

* * * *

At the stables, Regan stood hunched under the eaves. He seemed tense and unsettled.

"Has Rylee come home? She left my place pretty upset," Ash yelled, as he ran from his car.

Regan contemplated Ash with a quizzical look. "So she told you then?"

"To be honest I'm not sure what she told me. All I did was ask her to mind Lilli for a couple of days—I thought they would like the bonding time, but Rylee went crazy, hysterical, yelling at me she killed her brother and I shouldn't let her near Lilli. Then she stormed out the door. Is she here?"

"No. She's out there," Regan said pointing into the storm.

"Why? What the hell is going on? You're her brother—for God's sake fill me in."

"Rylee's scared to look after Lilli because she can't forgive herself for letting her baby brother wander off and drown in the river when she was twelve. Da has never forgiven her and she's afraid of seeing that same look in your eyes. She was terrified when you went ape at your sister after the accident. Rylee's been driving herself insane with worry ever since you told her you had a child."

"And this happened when she was twelve?" Ash asked, his voice sharp and shrill.

"Yes, just after our mother died. Rylee had been up all night nursing little Roisin with a fever. She fell asleep at the table. It was too late when she woke. They found Rohan an hour later, drowned. Da beat the hell out of her and turned his back on her. He would have thrown her out except the vicar interceded and said she was entitled to a home and one day, perhaps forgiveness. The forgiveness has never come," Regan stated baldly.

"And she takes the sole responsibility for that on her shoulders?" Ash asked.

Regan nodded. "She thinks you would never want Lilli in her care when you know what she did. She believes she killed her brother. She can't forgive herself."

"She was twelve, for God's sake—a child," Ash exclaimed.

Regan nodded. "Go find her, Ash, and bring her back."

"And damn it, I haven't helped by ranting and threatening anyone who might hurt Lilli. Poor sweet Rylee, what have I done to her?"

"Well, you better hope it isn't too late or you'll have me to deal with. I wasn't worried until the rain came down. Thor is unpredictable in stormy weather."

"Why haven't *you* gone to find her then?" Ash asked. Fear and urgent frustration surged through him at the little Irishman's laid-back manner. "Or don't you like to get your feet wet either."

Regan huffed his disgust at Ash's suggestion. "I have no mind about wet feet, Ashford St. Clair, but I'd be less than useless out there God damn it, I'm as blind as a bat in the dark."

"What?

"I have congenital night blindness, okay so now you know why the hell I'm still standing here instead of rescuing my sister. So you going to do something about it seeing you claim to love her so much?"

Ash tried not to resent Regan's sarcasm, the guy probably felt embarrassed admitting his impairment to a virtual stranger.

"Got a horse?" Ash asked.

Regan smiled. "Silly question. Monti's already saddled and he doesn't mind the wet. My oilskin is there and a first-aid kit is strapped behind the saddle. I think she went up the valley. Her favorite place is a small clearing just past the waterfall. She's probably just taken shelter under the cliffs, although it's not a good area to be in when it pours like this."

"I'll bring her back safe, Regan," Ash said as he climbed into the saddle.

The bay gelding was big and muscular and full of unleashed power. Taking a solid grip on the reins, Ash urged the horse into the pelting rain. The rain whipped in his face and the cold pervaded his bones, but he could think of nothing but the big horse carrying him forward, finding Rylee and knocking that unrealistic burden of guilt from her shoulders. And, given the chance, he'd knock it off her old man's shoulders too—or maybe his head. How dare he treat his own child like that? Then he pulled his thought up. He hadn't exactly been the perfect father either. He sighed. None of it mattered right now, except bringing Rylee home safe.

He slowed for the trees and let the horse make his own way. The stream had been transformed into a rushing river of muddy water and flailing debris. He urged the horse forward and, after a slight hesitation, he forded it without trouble. As they emerged on the far side, he heard a horse whinny. He peered through the driving gray curtain of rain. Thor stood with his back to the storm, huddled under one of the willows. Ash's heart lurched. Fear caught him in the chest and he gasped to draw breath. If Rylee had fallen—was hurt—he would never forgive himself. Thor was minus his saddle, but his bridle seemed intact. Ash left him under the tree.

He guided Monti upstream toward the waterfall. Any signs left by Rylee were long gone. Ash tried to keep his concern quiet in his chest. She was an experienced horsewoman. He shivered as the icy drops of rain trickled off his helmet and down the back of his collar. He had gloves on, but his hands were wet icy lumps, barely holding the reins. His jeans were soaked through, but Regan's riding boots kept his feet try. Monti made his way cautiously through the water, only flinching slightly when the lightning lit up the sky and thunder rumbled almost directly above them. Ash knew it was dangerous out here in an electrical storm, but he was not going home without Rylee.

"Rylee," he called again and again. His voice echoed back to him from the enclosing rock walls as if the spirits of the land were mocking him.

Then he heard it. A faint cry for help disembodied by the rain and scattered by the wind.

He urged Monti forward. "Rylee, where are you? Answer me," he shouted.

"Here, just around the second bend—to the left."

Her voice rose and fell, wavering and choked.

He rounded the bend and moments later found her huddled in a deep depression entangled in some sturdy roots. His heart leaped. She was safe. He climbed from the saddle, shocked at how stiff his legs were from the ride and the cold. He hobbled under the shelter and pulled her into a tight embrace. She was cold and wet, her hair hanging in tangled strands from under her helmet. A trickle of watery blood ran down her forehead. He grabbed the spare coat he'd brought and helped her into it before he pulled her back into his arms. She shivered violently and sagged against him.

"Oh, Rylee, I love you so. I was afraid something had happened to you," he shouted above the roar of the wind.

"I needed to think. I always come here. It's my special place," she shouted back.

"Did you come to any conclusions?"

"One, Ash. I cannot be stepmother to your child, and you wouldn't want me to be once I tell you the truth."

"I know what happened — Regan told me just now."

"And?"

"And, I'm not going to let you be crushed under such a burden — a burden you should not own. You were a mere child," he said close to her ear.

"But —"

He cut her words off, "No buts. I consider you more than capable of caring for my child and I'm going to enjoy teaching you the truth of that. Come on, my love. We need to get home."

She nodded and didn't resist when he released her and guided her toward the restive Monti. Her hands were freezing so he rubbed them before he pulled the dry gloves from his pocket on her and gave her the reins.

"Sit tight, love. I'll have you out of here soon."

"Poor Thor," she muttered.

"Thor's fine, sheltering under the willows."

It was a long, treacherous walk back down the gully. The flash flood had washed parts of the walls away and dug huge holes in the stream bed. Monti seemed to do a better job negotiating them than he did, stumbling several times and finally slipping into an icy pool of waist-high water. Ash watched Rylee huddled deep in the saddle. He could see she was shivering and blood still seeped from her head wound.

He sighed with relief when they rounded the bend and found Thor still standing forlornly under the willow.

"You all right, Rylee?"

She nodded. Ash scrambled aboard Thor and took up Monti's reins. The rain still slashed at them and periodically the sky was split by forks of white light, almost immediately accompanied by a growl of thunder that echoed in his bones.

Regan was waiting at the door when they arrived at the stables.

"Thank God, you're back safe, sis. I was so worried about you," Regan said as he reached up to help her down. "And you're bleeding, do you need the doc?"

"No, I'm all right, just a couple of scratches."

"Yeah, well I felt so bloody helpless..."

"It's okay, Regan."

Ash came up behind her and wrapped his arm around her. "Let's get you dry, love."

"Go on in, you two. Both of you need to get warm, before you get pneumonia. I'll see to the horses," Regan said.

They didn't argue. Ash swept Rylee up into his arms and trudged to the house. He kicked the door open and made his way under Rylee's direction to the en suite attached to her room. She stood there in her dripping clothes, watching him turn the shower on and adjust the temperature. Then he turned back to her, stripped her clothes off and dropped them in a pile on the floor before he pushed her under the steaming spray. She yelped when the hot water pelted against her icy skin, but she just stood there under the steaming spray. He tugged off his clothes, stepped into the shower and closed the door. He pulled her into his arms, suddenly acutely aware of his cock stiffening against her cold, wet skin. He embraced her, ignoring the demand of the fiery sexual desire that rushed over him at her closeness. With shower gel foaming between his palms, he massaged her with firm strokes trying to restore the warmth and circulation.

"I was so afraid for you, my love."

She peered up at him. "I thought I was going to drown in the flood. It came so quickly, without warning. I couldn't breathe and only those roots were stopping me being washed away. I thought of you and Lili and I cried because I thought I might never see you again." She tucked her arms around his neck and pressed closer to him. "Make love to me."

He didn't need to be told twice, already struggling with his arousal. She swept up some foam and lathered his chest, caressing sensuously down his muscular torso and over his hardened shaft. At her soft stroking, rampant need roared through him, making his cock stand out. His balls had relaxed in the warmth and when she cupped them and gently squeezed, the sensation was so exquisite it was almost unbearable. All he wanted to do was sink into her and have her body envelop him. He caressed her body and rubbed his hand between her thighs. Immediately she parted her legs to allow him access. The pubic hairs were a soft springy cushion on her mound and he cradled the soft swell with his hand before dipping in under the hooded flesh to find her clit. He eased his fingers into the wet, hot folds between her legs, gliding them up and down, caressing, exploring and finally halting at her opening. Boldly he inserted several digits into her tight, warm pussy. She shivered as he plunged in deeply then pulled out and thrust again. She clamped her muscles over his digits and whimpered her pleasure at his ministrations while he enjoyed the sensation of penetrating her body and feeling the walls of her vagina clutch at his movements. She moaned.

"I want more," she whimpered.

With her still held tightly against his chest, he eased her back against the maroon tiles where the water ran in glistening streams. He leaned against her, pressing her to the wall. She eased her legs apart and guided his cock to her opening. He almost exploded right then. He pushed into her, reveling in the feel of her heated flesh stretching to accommodate and enclose him. He sank deeper. She let out a muffled sob and brought her hips to his. He sank all the way and grunted at the magnitude of his pleasure. He sank into her again and again and she moved in unison with him. Her body was warm under his fingers, and she clung to him as she kneaded the muscles in his shoulders, whimpering her ecstasy with each movement. Her pussy quivered, so he picked up the pace and the quiver turned to undulating waves that tugged and pulled along his shaft. His own orgasm built fast and when she cried out, her head thrown back and her body arched, her muscles clenched around him then released. In the midst of her climax exploding around his cock, he slipped over the point of inevitability and throbbed with his own release, his hot fluid spilling into her. He groaned at the intensity of sensation that washed over him and he stilled, enjoying the warmth and closeness of their union.

"My love. My beautiful Rylee. So long wasted," he murmured and wrapped his arms around her, supporting her in the weakness of satiation. He pulled out of her, turned the water off and scooped her into his arms.

"Put me down. I can walk."

He ignored her protest, snatched up a towel then draped it around her. He laid her on the bed with tender care. With exquisite tenderness he dried her now-glowing skin. He did it slowly, inspecting every inch of her body, patting her scratches gently with antiseptic wipes then, with the lightest of touches, he massaged some bruise ointment into the sore bits already starting to color purple. He handed her some knickers and a bra then assisted her to put on several layers of clothing. He knelt and helped her put her slippers on. When he looked up, tears glistened on her cheeks.

"Don't cry, my love. There is nothing to fear anymore from the past."

She nodded. "I know."

With gentle fingers, he cleaned the gash on her forehead. "I don't think it needs stitches. It's more a scrape than anything." He placed a dressing over it. "Now turn around sideways and I'll dry your hair."

She didn't argue and after he had run the comb carefully through her curls, he turned the dryer on and slipped his fingers lightly through the silken tresses. He scooped up handfuls and blew the strands from his tender hold then he caressed her scalp, tussling the curls as he went. He felt the movement of

Rylee's body as she sighed. He smiled. She was enjoying this as much as he. The hardness already returning in his groin was a sensation he enjoyed, knowing he could satisfy his desire soon enough and the anticipation was delightful.

When her hair was dry, he turned the blower off. "I'm going down to organize dinner and light the fire. You come down when you're ready. Regan should be in soon. And I'll let Lilli know all is okay."

** * * *

With Lilli back to school, Ash was spending a lot of time at the stables. He helped her work the horses, especially getting Boomerang fit for his next endurance competition.

There was something very special about working the horses together side by side in the stables. Today they had had a breakthrough with Alsia, and Rylee was excited.

As she groomed the mare, she became aware of silence in the next stall. She sensed Ash wanted to say something important when he cleared his throat noisily. She stopped brushing Alsia and waited.

"I've been giving things some thought lately. I don't like the traveling involved in my business. I feel I'm letting Lilli down by not being here and I want to have a real family when we get married."

"But you haven't asked me yet, Ash," Rylee reminded him with a chuckle.

Ash sighed from the other side of the wooden divide. "I know, and I will. But first tell me what you think about me selling up and buying the place next door and me getting back into riding—both of us.

Together we could be one of the best outfits in Australia."

Ash popped his head above the wall. Rylee stared at him over the back of the mare. She didn't know what to say.

Ash frowned. "Well, say something, anything."

As he stared at her, a plethora of emotions played across his face—anxiety, excitement, fear, uncertainty.

"Yes," she said.

His mouth sagged open, then he smiled before he disappeared. With a clatter and a bang, he was beside her. Alsia shuffled away from his hurried entrance and snorted. Ash ignored the horse and swept Rylee into his embrace.

"You and me, living our dream. You do remember, ten years ago, what we planned."

"Yes, I remember."

"Well, it's not too late, my love—a bit different perhaps, but not less."

She nodded. He leaned closer and took command of her mouth. His kiss was hard and long, only ending when they were both gasping for air.

He pulled back from her. "It's agreed then. Now let's get these horses settled. I have other things on my mind."

Rylee giggled as he left the stall.

* * * *

The house was empty and silent when they returned.

"Can I stay over?" Ash asked. "I want to love you all night long."

She swung around into his embrace "You can stay the night, my love."

"Just the night?" he asked, tightening his hold on her.

"Forever, if you like," she murmured.

He leaned down and kissed her — a delicate kiss, full of promise. He embraced her in a tight clasp, and she wriggled her hips against his groin, thrilled at the instant response from his body before she took his hand and led him down the passage to her room. With the door barely shut behind them, Rylee fell into his arms, hungry to satisfy the fiery passion sparking inside her. Ash pushed Rylee's jumper and shirt up over her head, ignoring the buttons down the front and, moments later, she stood clad only in her lacy panties and bra. He scooped her up in his arms and walked her to the bed, his mouth clamped firmly onto hers. He laid her gently on mattress then stood back just out of reach. He gave her a lazy, seductive smile and flicked his hips slightly so they angled enticingly at her. She smiled back, knowing she would enjoy his little display.

He slowly undid the buttons on his shirt, revealing his broad chest with exquisite but frustrating slowness. She watched in fascination. Her body hummed with awareness as his masculinity was deliberately displayed in front of her. She licked her lips, flicking her tongue out the tiniest bit. His gaze was riveted on her face. She poked her tongue out more and slid it teasingly across her lips from one corner to the other. She saw him swallow in response, but he stayed in place. She breathed deeply, overwhelmed with the craving to touch his firm, warm skin. He turned suddenly, lowered his shirt off his shoulders and let it drop down his back as he wriggled his shapely backside at her. The firm mounds of his butt encased firmly in the imprisoning denim. His shirt dropped to the floor, and she watched him undo his belt and drag it slowly out of the belt loops. This, he cracked lightly in the air before he discarded it with a soft jingle. He wriggled his hips again to loosen his jeans from around his waist, and moments later, he pushed them slowly down over slim hips and the curve of his butt to reveal the waistband of white clinging Lycra pressed so close to his body. He let the jeans slide down his muscular thighs and land with a quiet plop on the floor. With a small side step, he untangled his ankles and kicked the jeans nonchalantly aside. As he turned to face her, she could see every outline of his genitals and studied his body—all of it—until finally she brought her gaze back to his rapidly swelling and stiffening cock. The white material hid nothing. He tucked his thumbs under his waistband but instead of exposing his throbbing penis, he turned his back to her once again and revealed the firm rounded flesh of his buttocks and the deep indentation between. Then he turned back and, with a flick of his finger, he uncovered his cock. It immediately jumped upright when he freed himself.

Rylee swallowed, trying to hold her need to jump him under control. He came to her then, naked and aroused. She undid her bra and slipped out of her panties before he joined her on the bed. Her skin sizzled with heat as it connected with his. She slid her palm over the hair on his chest and reveled in the sense of control as he lay back and let her explore. With bold strokes she trailed her hand down over his abdomen until she could cup the smooth softness of his balls. She massaged them gently before moving to the hot silken smoothness of his pulsating shaft. She wanted to suck him—to taste the saltiness of his pre-cum. She leaned in over him and licked the head of his cock with the tip of her tongue, then suddenly devoured the whole of his throbbing penis right to the base of the shaft. A deep grumble vibrated in his throat as he pressed himself into her. She slid her mouth up and down the hard, hot shaft before she concentrated on the head, curling her tongue around the base and dipping into the eye.

He pushed her away. "Stop, my love. I can't take any more."

As she reclined back against the pillows and parted her legs he lowered his head and proceeded to suck and lick every inch of flesh. When he finally came to her entrance of her pussy he probed inside with the tip of his tongue. She moaned in response to the pleasure that flooded through her in small, undulating ripples. Her heart thudded and her breath came in short little gasps. He eased himself on top of her and took command of her mouth, and she could taste herself on him as he thrust deeply inside her. She groaned at the pulsing ache sparked by him sliding his cock into her, stretching her, filling her. *God, how I want his loving, now and forever.* They moved in unison. Moments later, her body sizzled and hummed, the waves of her climax radiated through her body from where his cock was embedded in her. His rhythm matched hers. And the sensation built each time he dipped into her.

"Come for me, Rylee. My beautiful love." He moved faster, and she sensed his need to give in to his release. Her legs trembled as she sank into the undulations of her climax—hot, explosive and spiraling through her body. Even her hair ends tingled. She arched her back and moaned, clenching tightly around his stiffened shaft as it rammed into her. He thrust deeper, and grunted loudly before he stilled letting his release soar through him until she felt the heat of his cum deep inside. He collapsed on her, and she took his weight, feeling comforted by his closeness. When he finally did move, he rolled her with him then wrapped the quilt around them both.

His breathing slowly returned to a steady rhythm before he looked directly at her. "God, I've been such a blind fool."

"Don't beat yourself up about it. Arden is your baby sister after all. You wanted to believe the best of her, to support her in reaching her dreams, and there is nothing wrong with that. Deep down you're a good man, my love."

"But she lied…"

"Yes and you loved her. No one wants to face the fact that the person they care about is underhanded or off the rails."

He tucked his arms tighter around her. "Can you trust me, Rylee?"

"I want so much to trust you completely, but I'm still just a little afraid you will buckle under pressure from Arden."

"I've taken off the blinkers. I will *not* buckle. And now you have to do the same."

"What do you mean?"

Ash held out his hand toward her. "Stop seeing yourself as a failure in the mothering department. I've seen how you are with Lilli and I've talked to Regan. He loves and admires you so much. He says the family wouldn't have survived intact for those six years if it hadn't been for your sacrifice. He says all of them always believed they were loved and safe. Home to them was you."

She studied his hand, but made no attempt to take it. "It didn't feel like it at the time. I would hate to make a mistake with Lilli. She's not my child."

He moved closer to her and cupped her face before he kissed her lingeringly. "Shhh. I have seen you with my child and I have no doubts. A child needs to feel loved and safe then they will be fine, and I am sure you can do that and more, my love. Will you marry me? Will you make me and Lilli into a family?"

She hesitated for a short moment as terror washed over at the responsibility that came with the question, but she pushed it aside. She loved him and nothing else really mattered.

"Yes, Ash, I'll marry you, and yes, we will be a family — you, me and Lilli."

"Just, Lilli?" Ash asked with a cheeky grin.

A warm glow spread through her like rich red wine, and her face flushed with a mixture of pleasure and shyness. This man she loved so much wanted to have a child with her.

"Maybe not *just* Lilli, but I am not having twelve like my ma."

Ash chuckled as he buried his head between her breasts. She stroked his hair tenderly and stared up at the ceiling.

Even with Ash's expression of confidence in her mothering skills, she knew it would take time for her to feel truly comfortable being responsible for Lilli. At least with her fears and doubts out in the open she had nothing to fear if Roisin or her father said anything when — if — they came for the wedding. And she suspected mothering would get easier with practice. Her body began to hum and her thoughts scattered as she felt Ash's hand stroking between her legs.

* * * *

She stood at the door of the church, her heart fluttering erratically as she studied the people gathered there—their family and friends, even Arden. She lightly touched Lilli's shoulder and the child began her walk down the aisle, delicately casting pink rose petals on the floor. Regan grasped her arm in a firm grip and they stepped off together. The long silk train of her mother's wedding gown trailed out behind her as she walked toward her groom.

Ash stood tall and distinguished in a gray tuxedo. He smiled and her heart melted into a warm puddle. This was the man she loved, and tonight he would make love to her again and again until they were so sexually sated they couldn't move. Then she would tell him her secret—whisper in his ear about the child growing safely in her womb.

About the Author

Cassandra was a closet writer for several years before she got brave enough to share her work with anyone until she joined Eyre Writers Inc, a creative writing group in the seaside town of Port Lincoln and really began to improve.

Her first book was a 100,000 words family saga novel, but after a workshop on 'How to write a Mills and Boon', she embarked on a new direction—writing the romance novel.

After being made redundant from the job she loved in 2011 she became a carer for her frail, vision-impaired mother and turned to fulfilling her dream of becoming a writer.

When Cassandra's not writing she enjoys spending time with family and friends, especially her mother, and her three wonderful adult children and two adorable grandchildren.

She also enjoys egg decorating and carving, reading of course, painting and cooking.

Cassandra Hawke loves to hear from readers. You can find her contact information, website details and author profile page at http://www.totallybound.com.

Totally Bound Publishing